With two beautiful daughters, **Lucy Ryder** has had to curb her adventurous spirit and settle down. But because she's easily bored by routine she's turned to writing as a creative outlet, and to romances because— 'What else is there other than chocolate?' Characterised by friends and family as a romantic cynic, Lucy can't write serious stuff to save her life. She loves creating characters who are funny, romantic and just a little cynical.

Also by Lucy Ryder

Resisting Her Rebel Hero
Tamed by Her Army Doc's Touch
Falling at the Surgeon's Feet
Caught in a Storm of Passion

Rebels of Port St John's miniseries

Rebel Doc on Her Doorstep
Resisting Her Commander Hero

Discover more at millsandboon.co.uk.

RESISTING HER COMMANDER HERO

LUCY RYDER

MILLS & BOON

First published in Great Britain 2018
by Mills & Boon, an imprint of HarperCollins*Publishers*
1 London Bridge Street, London, SE1 9GF

Large Print edition 2018

© 2018 Bev Riley

ISBN: 978-0-263-07296-9

MIX
Paper from
responsible sources
FSC C007454

This book is produced from independently certified
FSC™ paper to ensure responsible forest management. For
more information visit www.harpercollins.co.uk/green.

Printed and bound in Great Britain
by CPI Group (UK) Ltd, Croydon, CR0 4YY

As always, to my family.
Especially my daughters Kate and Ash.
You are, and always will be, everything to me.

CHAPTER ONE

"LOWER THE BASKET!" yelled paramedic Francis Abigail Bryce into her headset over the whop-whop-whop of the helicopter hovering a hundred feet overhead. Wind and rain lashed at the ledge on which she was crouched, shielding the fallen climber.

If she slipped it was a long way down and probably wouldn't end well. It wasn't exactly how she'd envisioned spending her Friday evening but when word had come through from the rangers' station earlier that a climber had fallen, Frankie had been dispatched to the scene.

Further up the coast from the large seaside town of Port St. John's on the Olympic Peninsula in Washington state, heavy rains had caused a huge landslide and rescue teams were busy digging out survivors. With the storm wreaking havoc on the Juan de Fuca Strait, rescue personnel were stretched to the limit.

Frankie had returned with a few of the injured and then been the lucky candidate in the wrong place at the wrong darn time. Now, instead of providing emergency medical care at the site of the slide, she was clinging to a slick ledge only a few feet wide and a couple hundred feet from certain death because a group had thought it smart to go climbing in torrential rain.

She looked down into the guy's youthful face and shook her head. Probably a student on spring break, she thought. EMTs were always busy this time of the year, rescuing kids from their own ambitions.

"Hang in there, handsome," she yelled, aware that in the fifteen minutes she'd been there, he'd been slipping in and out of consciousness. She suspected a ruptured spleen and she'd already wrapped his leg in an inflatable compression cast.

Concerned about what was taking so long, Frankie looked up as a deep voice in her ear warned, "Heads up," and the next instant a large figure dropped onto the ledge. Dressed in a red and black jumpsuit and wearing a half-face helmet with comms mouthpiece, he looked like a huge bug from an alien world.

Frankie didn't need to see his eyes to know who it was. The hard, masculine jaw and the unsmiling line of his sensual mouth would have been a dead giveaway even if the hair on the back of her neck hadn't stood up like a freaked-out cat.

Nathan Oliver. The man who'd been back for months without at least letting her know he was home.

What the hell was he *doing here?* Wasn't he some super-secret commander of the Maritime Security Response Team or something? Unless her patient was a terrorist, or a foreign national in the country illegally—which Frankie doubted— she was pretty sure a member of the nation's deployable operations group stationed at Port St. John's wouldn't normally be part of search and rescue.

Then again, maybe the landslide and current conditions in the strait had put all coasties on call, including the MSRT. And, yeah, wasn't it just peachy that *he* had to be the one dropping from the sky?

Unhooking his line from the chopper, he gave

a couple of hand signals to the pilot above before his safety line disappeared into the lashing rain.

With her heart in her throat, Frankie ruthlessly squelched the urge to reach out and grab him before rotor wash blew him off the ledge. Or maybe before she gave him a little shove over the edge herself.

Okay, fine, so maybe she was tempted for about a nanosecond, but even though Nathan Oliver was the last person she wanted to see, she didn't want him to die either.

They'd meant too much to each other—once.

Besides, balanced on the rocky ledge and sure-footed and powerful as a mountain lion, Nate was more than capable of rescuing them both. He'd been a Navy SEAL before transferring to the Pacific North West unit of the US Coast Guard as Lieutenant Commander of the MSRT. Granted, the present conditions probably weren't the worst he'd experienced, but even *he* couldn't walk up sheer cliffs in this weather.

He dropped to his haunches beside her and she felt the sweep of his penetrating gaze. The resultant shiver, she told herself, was from being soaked through and freezing. It couldn't be that he still affected her.

That ship had sailed a lifetime ago and Frankie didn't make a habit of repeating her mistakes. Especially the very public ones that had devastated not only her pride but also her heart.

She saw his mouth form words that looked like, "You okay?"

But instead of replying, she yelled, "Where's the basket? He's going into shock."

He pointed skyward and she looked up to see the rescue litter swinging wildly in the gusting wind as it descended toward them. Nate barked out an order to the chopper and the pilot edged closer to the cliff face. But instead of controlling the swing, it caused the litter to spin.

He rose to his feet in one smooth move and stretched out a long arm to snag it. Almost in slow motion, Frankie watched as it abruptly shifted in the wind. She opened her mouth to yell a warning as the medevac litter flew through the air toward him.

He saw it coming too late to get out the way and it clipped him on the side of his helmet, sending him staggering backward toward the edge.

Time slowed and stretched, narrowing into an endless tunnel of pure horror as Nate fought to regain his balance. Then his foot slipped and in that split second before he went over, his gaze caught and held hers.

In that timeless instant, all the wild conflicting emotions she'd managed to suppress for twelve long years exploded through her, blinding her to everything but him.

Everything but the need to keep him from disappearing from her life forever. And before she realized she was moving, Frankie rose and leapt for him in one desperate move.

She reacted. As she always did.

Fear gave her strength and speed and before she could even process her actions, her icy fingers closed around his harness. Her momentum sent her thudding into him and Frankie wrapped her legs around him like a vice as they shot off the ledge.

Through the frantic yelling in the comms, she heard him curse as his arms enveloped her like banded steel. Her line went slack and for one awful moment she thought they were headed for the bottom of the gorge. She sucked in a breath, tightened her grip and pressed her face into Nate's throat, thinking stupidly that maybe it wasn't such a bad way to go.

Wrapped around his big tough body and with his uniquely potent masculine scent filling her lungs, Frankie could think of a dozen worse places to be.

It was the closest she'd been to him in twelve years. The closest she'd been since the night of her eighteenth birthday, the night he'd completely humiliated her in front of half the town.

He'd been around forever and as well as she'd thought she'd known him, she couldn't have known how much he'd changed or that he'd lost friends on his last mission. He'd looked the same—although bigger, harder and fitter—and acted the same as the boy she'd known her whole life. And if she'd noticed the closed-off expression in his eyes, the tight line of his mouth and jaw that night, she'd put it down to typical male arrogance and the fact that he was a member of the nation's elite fighting force, mixing with a bunch of wild immature teenagers all because she'd begged him to come to her party.

She should have known better than to try to

measure up to all the women in his life. To him she'd always just been his best friend's kid sister; wild, reckless—always wanting to tag along.

Besides, she'd never measured up, to him *or* to her brother Jack. At least not in her parents' eyes. Jack had been their golden child and Nate, popular, sporty and incredibly smart, was like their second son. They'd excelled at everything and it had been daunting, living in their shadow.

The birthday incident had been humiliating and she'd said things that filled her with guilt and shame whenever she thought about them. She'd lost him that day…and then seven years later she'd lost Jack in a mortar attack.

Her champions. Her own personal superheroes.

Frankie's heart squeezed. And now she and Nate were heading for the bottom of the gorge and she'd never get the chance to prove that she'd—

The safety line abruptly snapped taut, halting their graceful pendulum arc into empty space; halting the wild, regretful thoughts flashing through Frankie's mind. The next instant they were headed straight for the unforgiving rocky surface of the cliff face.

She tensed, because this was going to hurt.

Nate tried to turn, probably to take the brunt of the impact, but Frankie was attached to the safety line and the collision was hard enough to force the air from her lungs...and Nate's big warm muscular body between her thighs.

Stars exploded behind her eyes. Whether they were from the jolt to her skull or his hard, tough body, Frankie wasn't sure. But it was enough to rattle loose her good sense and cause some seriously inappropriate thoughts to flash through her mind, sending heat exploding through her body.

Nate Oliver was still the hottest man she'd ever known. The kind of hot that made women think inappropriate thoughts even while dangling hundreds of feet in the air by a slender nylon rope, and one wrong move away from falling to their deaths.

"Don't look down," he ordered. "And for God's sake don't let go. Not yet."

Of course Frankie didn't listen. Craning her neck, she looked down and then promptly wished she hadn't when a distressed squeak escaped without permission. All she could see beneath her was a dark cold emptiness. Vertigo abruptly clamped queasy fingers around her throat and her belly churned.

"Dammit, Frankie," Nate growled in her ear. "I said don't look down."

She wanted to tell him that he wasn't the boss of her but her breath was lodged in her throat and she could only gasp.

Oh, God. How mortifying. Inside, Fearless Frankie—Port St. John's former wild child—was freaking out.

"I'm going to let you go," Nate said calmly, and it took a couple of beats for his words to register.

When they did, she snapped, "No!" and tightened her grip on him. No way was he letting go.

"Just enough to free my hands and feet," he explained quietly. "Then I'm going to crab-walk us to the ledge. Okay?"

She wanted to say no, but she knew it would take a little strain off the safety line and keep it from shearing off on the rocky outcroppings.

She really, *really* didn't want that to happen.

She looked up at the suspended medevac litter, which was now hanging motionless a few feet to her left.

Go figure.

Gritting her teeth, she nodded jerkily, tightening her grip on Nate's harness. Her thighs clenched around him until they ached, and all she could think was, *Thank God for all those squats and lunges I've been doing lately.*

"Good girl," he murmured, and she wanted to snort because she was about as far from being a good girl as they were from the ground. He eased his grip until all that kept him from succumbing to the law of gravity were her arms and legs.

He murmured into his comms and then with his feet planted flat against the cliff face, he began to move them toward the ledge.

It couldn't have been more than a minute since Frankie's spectacular leap off the edge but her muscles had begun to shake and she didn't know how much longer she'd be able to hold on.

Beneath Nate's jumpsuit, muscles bunched and flexed, giving her a few more inappropriate thoughts. Thoughts that might have freaked her out if she hadn't been closer to death than she liked. Frankly, in the circumstances, she figured she was allowed.

Besides, it had been so long since she'd had inappropriate thoughts of any kind that she might as well enjoy them. They were the closest she'd had to actual sex in forever.

Finally, the tension on her harness lessened and Nate straightened, big feet planted shoulder width apart.

After a couple of beats he said, "You can let go now, Francis," the dry tone as much as his use of the hated name bringing her head up. The first thing she saw was his mouth, beautifully sculpted and much too tempting.

Tearing her gaze away, she looked up into eyes as dark and fathomless as the death they'd just escaped. Sometime in the past couple of minutes—probably while she'd been having those hot thoughts—he'd lifted his visor and the warmth in his usually unreadable gaze stunned her.

"You okay?" His mouth was barely an inch away and all it would take was one tiny move from her and—

Spooked, Frankie flashed a quick look to the left and saw they were once more on the ledge. Her patient, wrapped in a silver emergency blanket, was a few feet away, waiting for her to get her act together.

"I'm fine," she croaked, her throat desert dry

and tight with tension while adrenaline still pumped through her at their near disaster.

Eager to put a little distance between them, Frankie released the stranglehold she had on him and slid to the ground until all that connected them were her fingers still locked on his harness.

"Francis."

She opened her mouth in a snarled protest but it gave her the impetus she needed to let him go. She might have pushed away from him if they hadn't been perched on a narrow, slick ledge and she hadn't just taken a decade off her life with that one daring leap.

"You good?" he asked again, ducking his head to look into her eyes. He must have been reassured because he didn't wait for her to reply. "Help me secure the PEP so we can get off this ledge."

Frankie shook her head even though she knew he meant the patient extrication platform. Sucking in a shaky breath to still the churning in her gut, she shoved all her messy emotions aside and got her head in the game. She had a patient who needed her undivided attention and the litter swaying gently just over their heads was waiting to airlift him to the closest trauma center.

Everything else could wait. Including her freak-out because no way was anyone witnessing that.

Within minutes, they'd transferred the student to the backboard and strapped him into the litter. Nate then reattached the hoisting strapline and with a hand signal from him, Frankie's patient rose into the air. She watched as hands reached out to snag the litter and pull it aboard the chopper before expelling the breath she'd been holding.

Litter rescues occasionally went bad but, despite the rocky start that had almost cost Nate his life, this one had gone relatively smoothly. But she wanted to be off the ledge before something else went wrong. Before she lost the tight grip on her emotions.

She wasn't looking forward to climbing back the way she'd come either. Her arms and legs shook, which would make the ascent a little tricky even though the rangers at the top had set up a standing body belay and would take most of her weight as she "walked" up the cliff face.

She'd wait until Nate left with the chopper before attempting the ascent for fear of completely humiliating herself any further.

Out of the darkness the hoisting strapline appeared again and Frankie let out a tiny relieved breath. Any minute now she'd be free to fall apart without an audience.

She watched Nate catch the metal connector clip and murmur something that she couldn't quite catch. Now would be a good time for Fearless Frankie to regain control, she thought, because smartass and cocky was way better than cowering, trembling and freaked out.

She gave a cocky grin and quipped, "So long, soldier," adding a snappy salute for good measure.

"It's *sailor*, not soldier," he growled, as he unclipped her line and gave it a quick tug.

"What are you *doing*?" she snapped in outrage, making a grab for it, but it was already out of reach as the rangers above reeled it in. She turned on him with a snarled "Are you insane?" but he ignored her, snapping her onto his harness capture strap. Of course, she tried to stop him but he brushed her hands aside with a quick impatient flick and hooked them both to the hoisting line.

Eyes on hers, he wrapped his arms around her and said, "Trust me."

The words had her heart lurching as the truth landed like a punch to the solar plexus. God, she did. Didn't want to…but did.

"No," she lied, but he must have read the reluctant truth in her eyes because he said, "Bring us in, Boom," and the next instant they were airborne.

Frankie swallowed as they swung away from the ledge. She didn't like the feeling of being suspended in a sea of blackness while wind, rain and rotor wash lashed at them from every side any more than she liked being vulnerable.

To *any*one…let alone this man.

She'd tried it once and he'd devastated her, stomping on her tender heart with his size thirteen tactical boots. It was the last time she'd allowed her feelings to show.

"I'll get you for this, soldier," she warned through clenched teeth and squeezed her eyes closed against the overwhelming pull of the man pressed intimately against her.

Gone was the cocky, handsome boy who'd treated her with all the indulgent impatience of an older sibling. In his place was a man whose powerful cocktail of tightly coiled testosterone and simmering pheromones was even more treacherously compelling.

Even the expression in his eyes was different—sometimes intense, sometimes brooding but always distantly watchful.

This Nate might look like an older, hotter and harder version of the boy she'd once loved but somewhere along the line he'd acquired a darkness that made him more than dangerous, more than lethal, to women everywhere.

Over the sound of the chopper she heard him yell, "You falling asleep there, spider girl?"

Her eyes popped open and she looked up to see the red and white fuselage looming closer. A couple of visored men watched and controlled their ascent, reminding Frankie of a movie she'd seen about alien abduction.

"No," she muttered. "I'm pretending I'm on a beach in Hawaii."

He must have heard because his mouth kicked up at one corner and before she could fully grasp the sudden transformation, hands were reaching for them, pulling them in. The instant she felt the capture strap release, Frankie scrambled over to where a crewman was tending her patient and wondered what she thought she was doing, because she had a feeling that getting sucked into Nate Oliver's force field again...would be an unmitigated disaster.

Fortunately, she was too smart to let that happen. *Way* too smart.

Her patient's eyes were open but he appeared dazed and disorientated. "Focus on me, handsome," she yelled over the noise of the engine, and quickly freed his arm to set up an IV. "You hang in there, okay?"

Looking up briefly to gauge their ETA, she noticed several pairs of eyes on her and became aware of the grins.

Frowning, she looked around and caught sight of Nate's expression and by the firm unsmiling line of his sexy mouth, he wasn't happy. But then again—apart from that flash of wry humor—unsmiling seemed to be his default expression.

At least when it came to her.

Her belly clenched.

"What?"

"*Yowza*, lady," a crewman yelled, his wide

toothy grin and smooth cheeks all she could see beneath the bug helmet. "You saved Sammy in the most awesome move I ever saw. Ever think of joining the circus?"

Sammy? she thought with a frown. *Who the heck is Sammy?*

Thinking maybe they were talking about her patient, Frankie drawled, "I'm allergic to rings," laughing when she was rewarded with confused looks. She shook her head. "Never mind."

No way was she explaining that one. She'd decided a long time ago that marriage wasn't for her and guys seemed to think all a woman wanted was a wedding ring and a white picket fence.

Determinedly pushing aside unpleasant thoughts, Frankie willed the chopper to move faster through the air. The sooner they arrived at the hospital, the sooner her patient could be rushed into surgery. And she *really* needed to escape this inexorable pull Nathan appeared to still have on her double-X chromosome.

CHAPTER TWO

HOURS LATER FRANKIE dragged her weary feet through the ambulance bay doors into ER. The adrenaline had long since faded and she was feeling every strained muscle and ache as though she'd been through a marathon workout session.

Fortunately, the mud slide hadn't been as extensive as everyone had feared and most people had managed to escape the worst of it. Those that hadn't had already been admitted or treated and released.

It had probably been the longest shift of her career. Her jumpsuit clung wetly to her skin and her boots squelched with every step. There was also something wrong with her back that she could no longer ignore. She'd check it herself but one of her superpowers wasn't the ability to make her arms bend the wrong way or her head swivel like an evil toy in a horror movie.

Fortunately, the ER was quiet after the earlier

rush and she found the person she was looking for in the staff lounge, stuffing her face with one donut while searching through the bakery box for another.

Paige Carlyle looked as exhausted as Frankie felt. At the sound of the door opening, the petite doctor looked up guiltily—cheeks bulging like a chipmunk's—as though she'd been caught doing something illegal.

"Those things will kill you," Frankie announced, snagging the full to-go mug off the counter. She swallowed a large mouthful and grimaced. "And so will this."

"Hey," Paige objected around a mouthful of pastry, and snatched the cup away, cradling it protectively against her chest. "It's hot, delicious and I need the sugar."

"No, you don't. You need some veggie juice and a nice long soak in a hot tub."

Paige made a face at the mention of veggie juice. "Yuk, I'm not drinking pond scum," she declared, gleefully washing down her donut with hot chocolate and making sounds that were a little too disturbing in Frankie's opinion. Paige reluctantly closed the bakery box and slumped against the counter. "But a long hot soak sounds like heaven. My feet hurt and I haven't been home in so long Ty's probably forgotten what I look like."

"Stop whining. It's unattractive," Frankie said with an accusing frown. "And so are your constant reminders that you have a sexy hunk waiting for you with home-cooked meals and daily massages."

Paige's mouth curved in a secretive smile and she made another sound that ratcheted Frankie's irritation level a couple of notches. "You sound jealous," Paige observed mildly. "Like you want a sexy hunk at home too."

Frankie snorted. "Who doesn't?"

"Well, I do know another unattached sexy hunk you might be interested in," the doctor said craftily.

"Your brother? The air force top gun?" Frankie gave a dramatic sigh. "He's hot and I just *love* a man in uniform."

Paige gagged. "Yuk. *No.* I was talking about someone in another sector of the armed forces. Say…the Coast Guard?"

"Not interested," Frankie said promptly. "And

I can handle my own love life, thanks." Or lack thereof, she reminded herself dryly. "You just concentrate on Terrible Ty."

Tyler Reese had been Nate and Jack's best friend until the summer they'd turned eighteen. Something had happened that had landed the three friends in a lot of trouble and it had been the last time Ty had been in Port St. John's— except for Jack's funeral—until an injury had threatened to end his surgical career. He'd returned to recuperate and had run into Paige on his first night.

Or rather into Paige's flashlight, which had clearly knocked some sense into him because he'd left his life and big city career to move north.

Paige cleared her throat and stared at Frankie expectantly. "Is there something you need to tell me, Ms. Bryce?" she asked with excruciating politeness.

Frankie frowned at her friend's tone. "No," she said warily, and when the doctor just narrowed her eyes, she shrugged and couldn't stop the sharply indrawn breath at the movement.

Paige must have seen something in her expression because she demanded, "What did you do?"

Of course Frankie answered with an affronted "Nothing," hoping Paige would drop it because the doctor looked like she needed a break as much as Frankie did. She'd just go home, have a hot shower and fall into bed. She could deal with everything after about twelve hours of shut-eye.

Paige scoffed. "Tell me before I call Ty." She paused and her gaze turned crafty. "Or better yet, maybe I'll call a big bad coastie. He can hold you down while I examine you." Knowing exactly who Paige was talking about, Frankie narrowed her eyes dangerously but her expression clearly didn't intimidate the medical center's newest specialist.

"Let's go," Paige said, tossing her to-go cup in the trash before moving toward the door, turning impatiently when Frankie didn't move. "Well? What are you waiting for?"

"An ER physician?"

Paige rolled her eyes because everyone knew that though she was a qualified pediatrician, she was still paying off her state-granted tuition by working in ER. "Your smart mouth doesn't intimidate me, Ms. Bryce," she drawled. "Room

Four. Stat," she ordered, before disappearing through the door.

Frankie closed her eyes, her boots rooted to the spot. It wasn't that she was being deliberately difficult. She was just too tired to move. Oh, yeah, and every breath reminded her of her flying trapeze stunt. Moving required skills she'd temporarily misplaced.

A second later the door opened again and Paige stuck her head inside, scowling when she saw that Frankie hadn't moved. She narrowed her gaze and gave her cellphone a peremptory waggle. "Now," she snapped.

Frankie frowned. "Does Ty know how annoying you are?"

"Of course he does," she announced cheerfully. "It's one of the things he loves about me."

Frankie rolled her eyes because Paige was right. Ty did love her. His feelings for the pint-sized Attila the Hun were so obvious that it made Frankie just a little bit jealous.

She wanted someone to look at *her* like that.

Sighing, because now she was feeling sorry for herself, she followed Paige down the passage into an empty ER room.

"Okay," the doctor said with her hands on her hips. "What hurts?"

Finding levity in the situation, Frankie snorted and reached for the zipper tab on her jumpsuit. "Maybe you should ask what doesn't hurt...and go from there?" Maybe she should have gone home before she tried this because there was no way she was going to be able to dress again without bawling like a baby.

Paige pulled on a pair of surgical gloves and studied her. "Lemme guess. You acted rashly during that mountain rescue and you've hurt your back."

"What mountain rescue? How do you know it's my back?" Frankie demanded irritably. "And I'm never rash—at least, not any more—and not unless I need chocolate. Then all bets are off."

Paige arched her brow. "It's the way you're holding yourself." She leveled a mildly irritated yet softly understanding look that made Frankie squirm. "And I know you hate being a burden because you harbor what you think is a super-secret need to make amends for your past, Frankie. So you were wild and rebellious." She shrugged impatiently. "Big deal. We all do dumb stuff when we're kids."

Frankie spluttered. "That's ridiculous. I bet you—"

But Paige interrupted with, "You're an excellent paramedic—the most advanced one on the coast, actually—but maybe you should think about saving yourself."

"What does *that* mean?" Frankie demanded with a scowl.

"It means no woman is an island. It means that you should accept help once in a while. Now would be good...while we're both still standing." Paige huffed out a laugh when Frankie rolled her eyes. She reached out to peel the jumpsuit off Frankie's shoulders and had barely got it halfway down her arms before sucking in a sharp breath.

"Ooh, that's nasty."

"What?" Frankie demanded, craning her neck at the tone in Paige's voice. "What?"

"You really should have had this seen to ages ago," Paige scolded, and gently pulled Frankie's wet undershirt away from her back. Frankie must have made a sound because Paige cursed. "Did this happen before or after your Fearless Frankie stunt?"

"I don't know what you're talking about."

"Sure you do, since everyone *else* knows about it," Paige groused. "And how come I have to hear via the grapevine that you made a superhero save, anyway? I thought best friends told each other everything?"

Not everything…because there were some things a person didn't share. With anyone. Especially things that made Frankie cringe with shame whenever she thought about them.

Paige huffed and eased Frankie's bloodied tank top over her head, leaving her in a black sports bra, jumpsuit pooled at her waist. She made a sound of exasperation at what she'd uncovered. "I know we joke about it but, Frankie, really, taking a flying leap off a ledge? What the heck were you thinking?"

Wincing as Paige gently probed a particularly tender spot, Frankie demanded, "Who told you about that?"

"So it's true?"

She sighed irritably. "It's complicated… *Ouch.* That hurts."

"Not as much as it's going to," Paige said shortly. "But seriously? It's like you have a death wish or something." Frankie opened her mouth to object but Paige beat her to it with a snapped-out "I'm busy here." But after a couple of beats she said almost absently, "There's bruising, a couple of lacerations and some bad grazing. What really happened?"

Frankie gave a negligent shrug. "I got caught between a rock and a hard place." Paige sighed and began cleaning Frankie's injuries. "Wanna tell me about it?"

"No," Frankie said.

At the same time a deep voice drawled from the door, "Yes, Francis, let's hear all about it."

She closed her eyes wearily and thought, *Not now. Not ever.* Or at least not while she was feeling exhausted and raw and couldn't think of a snappy comeback.

She'd hoped to avoid the lecture she knew was coming but she should have known he would eventually hunt her down. He'd hunted terrorists for a living, for God's sake. What had made her think she could continue to evade him?

She'd only managed to avoid him since the

night of her eighteenth birthday because he'd wanted it that way. She'd wanted it too, she reminded herself, mostly to forget that the boy she'd idolized had called her a selfish willful brat who didn't think about how her actions affected others. He'd also called her reckless and told her to grow up.

Then he'd left town. Getting as far away from her as possible.

Well, she was cool with that. *Really* cool, she thought fiercely. She just wished he'd stayed away.

Turning, she eyed him with what she hoped was cool disinterest, ignoring the fact that even after the long night, he looked bigger, badder and hotter than ever.

While she looked like a complete mess.

Go figure.

"This is a medical examination room," she said flatly. "Only medics allowed."

One dark brow rose in silent challenge. "Want to call Security, Francis?" he drawled with a hint of amusement that did nothing but raise her blood pressure. And not in a good way.

"No," she snapped, because he had awesome

SEAL skills no security team could match. "I don't want any witnesses when I use a scalpel." Her unspoken, *on you*, hung in the air between them.

It had genuine amusement lighting his eyes and curling his mouth in a smile that had *her* gritting her teeth in aggravation. Arrogant BAB, she snarled inwardly, using the acronym she and Paige had thought of one night when they'd been a little tipsy. But "badass boy" fitted Nate like a pair of snug boxer briefs. Except seeing him now, it was clear he was no longer a boy.

"You thinking of taking me on, Francis?" he drawled smoothly, his gaze hot and intense one moment, dark and unreadable the next. The lightning-fast changes left her confused and more than a little irritated.

"You think I can't?" she challenged, furious with the shiver crawling up her spine that had nothing to do with Paige using alcohol swabs on her scrapes and cuts.

Besides, taking him on while she was tired and hurting wouldn't be smart. Not to her pride and certainly not to her heart.

She glared at him. Why couldn't he take his sexy self off and leave her alone?

"You can try." He smirked with typical male arrogance that had Frankie barely restraining herself from snarling.

Casually propping his shoulder against the door frame as though he had every right to be there, Nate locked his dark brooding eyes on his hapless target—*her*—his sensual mouth an uncompromising and disapproving line. All humor had gone.

Frankie shivered. Yeesh. She'd forgotten that about him, about his ability to focus so intently on a person they felt like the most important person in the world. Like they were under a microscope.

She turned away to stare at a wall chart without seeing a thing. But her body, the traitor, was locked like a tractor beam on him. And then... and then her nipples tightened and tingles spread across her skin like a heat rash that she blamed on the fact that she was cold and wet.

"Excuse me, *Doctor*," she drawled, ignoring the hunk in the doorway. "But isn't there a rule that says only family members are allowed in an ER room?"

Paige sent Nate a quick look and muttered something that sounded like, "Don't pull me into whatever is between you two."

Frankie felt guilty for about two seconds. She didn't want to involve Paige but she wasn't above using her friend as a buffer either. Especially when it came to Commander Cool.

"There isn't anything to get between," she said smoothly, ignoring Nate and mentally celebrating the complete disinterest in her tone.

"Frankie." Paige protested her rudeness, but Frankie ignored the rebuke, watching Nate out of the corners of her eyes while pretending to ignore him too. For long moments he studied her until she was ready to start squirming.

Finally, with a casual roll of his shoulder, he pushed away from the door frame.

"It's all right, Doc. I'll go." A big hand landed palm flat against the door in preparation of pushing it open. He paused and with a hard look at Frankie said to Paige, "For you."

Meaning he'd never do it for Frankie. The notion stung, and before she could stop it, hurt sliced through her. Quickly squelching it with the full force of her will, she reminded herself that getting her feelings hurt by Nate's attitude would not only be stupid but self-defeating. Besides, she was over her silly adolescent infatuation and the last thing she needed or wanted was someone with a hero complex.

She turned and locked gazes with him just as he pushed open the door. His mouth twisted with faint irony and the next instant he was gone.

Heavy silence descended on the room but Frankie could literally feel her friend vibrating with questions and maybe a bit of exasperation. She slid a sidelong look at her and caught Paige chewing on her lip. She could practically see the wheels spinning away in the brunette's head and counted the seconds until the other woman cracked.

She reached nine.

"Seriously, Frankie?" Paige finally burst out. "You blew him off? Are you sick, dumb or just insane? And what the heck is going on between you two anyway?" she continued, without waiting for a reply.

"Nothing." Frankie sighed, tension draining

abruptly and leaving her beyond exhausted. "Nothing I want to talk about anyway. But I am confused about why everyone keeps referring to Nathan as Sammy."

Paige was silent for a couple of beats as she studied Frankie. She must have decided not to probe because all she said was, "It's his coastie handle."

"Handle?"

Paige rolled her eyes. "His nickname, his moniker."

"I know what a handle is, Dr. Cutie," Frankie said, because she knew *that* moniker irritated Paige. Besides, why should she be the only frustrated person in the room? "I'm just not sure I understand this one."

Paige shrugged and swabbed a particularly tender spot that had Frankie sucking in a sharp breath.

"I'm guessing it might have something to do with him transferring from the SEALs." She sprayed her back with iodine. "Lie down, will you? I need to put in a few stitches."

Frankie's gut clenched. "Can't you just glue them or something?"

"No. I can't."

"But—"

"I know you, *Francis*," Paige briskly interrupted when Frankie opened her mouth to argue. "The first thing you're going to do when you get home is ignore doctor's orders and shower. Next thing you know you're back here with an infection. Besides, I'll make sure they're small and won't leave any scars."

Her mouth snapped shut. Okay, so maybe Paige did know her. "Fine." She lay facedown on the bed and propped her chin on her stacked hands. At some point she must have dozed off because the next thing she knew, Paige was tapping her arm.

"All done, sleeping beauty," she said cheerfully, "and before you object, I've booked you off for a few days. Now go home and get some sleep. No picking up heavy objects or taking flying leaps off ledges. And absolutely no physical activity or you'll undo all my hard work."

Frankie sat up with a yawn and twisted to see Paige's handiwork but her back was a patchwork of waterproof dressings. She tentatively rolled her shoulders to test her flexibility and was pleasantly surprised to discover that, though it pulled a little, it didn't hurt.

"While you were snoring, I gave you a shot of pain meds and antibiotics," Paige said, clearing up the mystery. "You should be good till the morning."

"Which is in about an hour," Frankie said, sliding off the bed and blinking blearily at her wristwatch. "How long was I out?"

"About twenty minutes." Paige helped Frankie pull her jumpsuit up her arms and over her shoulders. "I'd let you sleep but Andrews is in charge tonight."

Frankie brushed her hands away.

"I can dress myself, Mom, thanks."

Paige backed off with a snicker and picked up a clipboard. She scribbled something then looked up. "Are your tet shots up to date?" Frankie grunted out a reply that the doctor must have understood because she tore a sheet off a pad and held it out. "I've prescribed antibiotics and pain meds. Get them. With all that bruising, you're going to be sore in the morning."

Frankie mustered a snappy salute. "Thanks,

Doc," she said, and with a quick hug headed stiffly for the door. "You're the best."

"Yes, I am." Paige chuckled. "Just be sure to put that in the patient survey on your way out."

Frankie stopped abruptly at the door when she remembered their earlier visitor. She wouldn't put it past Nate to hang around and ambush her while she was spaced out on pain meds and couldn't defend herself.

"What's wrong?" Paige asked, alarmed. "Are you hurt somewhere else?"

Shaking her head, she quickly stepped aside and nudged Paige into the doorway. "Tell me what you see. Go on," she urged when her friend looked at her like she was a crazy person on the verge of a meltdown.

When she made a get-on-with-it gesture, Paige gave a dramatic eye-roll and stuck her head out, looking around with dramatic furtiveness. "What am I looking for?" she whispered loudly, clearly enjoying the cloak-and-dagger moment.

Frankie growled and pulled her back into the room. "Any...um...*thing* that doesn't belong in the ER?"

Paige's eyes widened and sparkled with enjoyment. "You mean like a…a seal?"

"No." *Of course a SEAL.* She huffed out an exasperated laugh, both at herself and Paige.

"Well, no sign of seals or any other wildlife," Paige said with a quick head-shake.

"Okay, good. Because I'm not in the mood to fend off any marine mammals or any other wildlife."

She wasn't in the mood to deal with Nate, especially not in his disapproving big-brother role.

No wait, she amended. Not in any role. She just wanted to go home, shower for about an hour and then fall into bed and sleep for a week.

"Thanks, Paige, I owe you," she said quietly, and walked stiffly from the room.

"Yes, you do, Francis Abigail," Paige said, popping her head into the passage. "And I plan to collect…in the form of an explanation. About sea mammals."

"Sure," Frankie said agreeably. "I know a lot about whales and dolphins." She smirked when Paige sighed loudly, but no way was she sharing her humiliation at the hands of Nathan Oliver. She'd never told a living soul about what had really happened that night and had no intention of discussing it now.

Or ever. Even with her best friend.

CHAPTER THREE

LIEUTENANT COMMANDER NATHAN OLIVER leaned against the wall in the dark and drank from a disposable cup. He hadn't wanted the sweet, black coffee but it was warming his hands and keeping him awake while he waited for the one woman on the face of the planet with the ability to drive him completely nuts.

Nate hunched into his wet-weather Coast Guard jacket and blinked his gritty eyes. He was cold, wet and exhausted after a thirty-hour shift and wasn't in any kind of mood to deal with Frankie. But it needed to be done before her stupid recklessness got her killed. Besides, being cold, wet and exhausted was nothing compared to what he'd survived in the teams. Nothing compared to what *could* have happened up in the mountains.

But last night wasn't what he wanted to think about; he got icy chills just recalling the expression of horror on Frankie's face as she'd risen to her feet and launched herself at him in that split second before he'd gone over.

From experience, he knew the memory would be replaying in an endless loop for weeks, if not months, to come. His belly cramped into a tight ball and he felt a dull pain in his chest—right next to his heart. Massaging the ache, he reminded himself that he wasn't having a coronary.

It was probably just indigestion from having to drink hospital coffee.

And since it was her fault he was drinking the swill, he added it to her already lengthy list of transgressions. Transgressions that included keeping him from his warm bed, acting without thinking and…and being all grown up and too damn beautiful for her own good.

Okay, and maybe for his good too, but no way would he ever admit that out loud…or go there. Not with her. Not after he'd promised Jack that he'd look out for his wild and willful kid sister if anything happened to him. Only Frankie was no longer a kid; something he'd been forcibly reminded of when he'd walked into that ER room.

Nate sucked in a breath at the memory of her sitting there, her back a patchwork of bruises, scrapes and lacerations. Injuries she'd sustained when she'd gone all Queen of the Jungle and saved his ass.

In that moment he'd wanted to grab her and shake some sense into her but the sight of her had hit him like a bullet to the chest. Gone was the wild skinny tomboy…in her place was a tall, stunning beauty with lush curves in all the right places.

Frankie was all grown up.

But the last thing he wanted to notice was… that. Besides, she'd been like a sister to him. And then there was the blood oath he and Jack had made the day they'd left to join the armed forces.

He was going to honor that promise, preferably from afar, but right now he needed to make her see that her actions had been reckless, thought-less and dangerous.

He'd had every intention of doing it last night but they'd been surrounded by people and she'd been playing "evade and escape" since touch-ing down on the hospital helipad. It was a game they'd been playing since his return to Port St. John's. A game he was beginning to tire of.

Granted, after that first week when he'd sur-

prised Frankie chatting with his mother and sister
in their kitchen, he'd deliberately kept his distance, needing to deal with being back in Port
St. John's and his new MSRT commission. He'd
also had his hands full, helping his mother cope
after a climbing accident had left his sister, Terri,
a paraplegic.

He'd never admit it, but he'd also been having nightmares about the last SEAL mission that
had taken the lives of several teammates. Bleeding from his own injuries, he'd tried to rescue
his fallen buddies but he'd been pinned down.
Waiting for air support, all Nate had been able to
think about had been the wild grief in Frankie's
eyes at Jack's funeral and wondering if she would
grieve for him if he was killed in action.

The wild jumble of emotions had terrified him
and he'd done what any man did when dealing
with stuff he didn't know how to handle. He'd
shoved everything deep and stayed away. Partly
because she would have prodded and poked until
he'd told her all his dark secrets and revealed his
pain and feelings of failure. But mostly because,
well…he didn't trust himself around her because
she drew him in as no other woman did.

His mother swore Frankie had changed since her wild adolescence days but Nate wasn't so sure. That crazy stunt was exactly what the wild child would have done in the past. And damn the consequences.

His jaw clenched when he imagined what those consequences would have been if she hadn't been hooked to a lifeline. She would have plummeted to her death with him.

What kind of reckless fool did that?

But even as the thought occurred, he knew. It was the kind that put someone else's life ahead of their own. The fiercely loyal kind that had your back; no questions asked—no matter what. The kind he'd known only in his best friends Jack and Ty, and then his buddies in the teams.

Yet, without hesitation, she'd dived off a slippery ledge to save him. In spite of everything he'd done to push her away.

Scowling down at the rapidly cooling contents of his cup, Nate wondered if he was punishing Frankie for all his confusing emotions. A prickle of warning tightened the back of his skull and his head came up just as the very woman he'd been thinking about sauntered through the automatic doors. Francis Abigail Bryce. His best buddy's sister. The wild, exuberant girl he'd watched over for too many years while growing up—and had spent a further twelve trying to forget.

Sucking in a slow deliberate breath, Nate pushed away from the wall and willed his body to relax, his mind to calm. It was a trick he'd learned in the teams. A trick that helped him focus only on the mission ahead while ignoring everything else.

Dealing with Frankie was guaranteed to be as dangerous, as unpredictable and explosive as any of the classified missions he'd survived.

Without taking his eyes off her artfully messy red-gold hair, he threw the rest of his coffee into the bushes and tossed the cup in the nearest trash bin.

He was about to head after her when the door burst open and a young medic ran out, only to stop abruptly when she saw him. "Nate," Paige said breathlessly. "Th-thank God."

Despite his impatience, Nate paused and eyed his best friend's fiancée. "Problem, Doc?"

"Yes," she huffed worriedly, craning her neck and squinting into the darkness. "She shouldn't be driving. I was just about to go wrestle her into my car so she didn't have to drive home but I'm on duty."

"What I wouldn't give to see that?" he drawled, leaning forward to plant a quick kiss on her forehead. "Don't worry, Paige. I've got this."

"Are you sure, Nate? Because Frankie is—"

"I'm sure, Doc," he interrupted gently. "Don't worry, I'll get our girl home safely." And with his hands shoved into his pockets, he took off into the darkness, not about to admit that he still thought of her that way.

Our girl.

How many times had he, Jack and Ty said the same thing? *What's our girl up to now? Surely our girl wouldn't be so reckless as to dive off Devil's Point into the sea?*

He caught up with Frankie in the far corner of the car park where she'd parked her battered SUV. He'd trawled the parking earlier and deliberately found a space a couple of cars down from her vehicle so she couldn't sneak off.

He knew the instant she became aware she was being followed when her stride faltered, so imperceptibly he would have missed it if he hadn't been a trained observer. Or watching her long shapely legs.

She stiffened and, without turning, said, "Go home, soldier." As though she knew who it was before he could announce himself.

"We need to talk," he said, ignoring her continued use of the "soldier" moniker. She was determined to annoy him and Nate was just as determined not to be riled. He'd decided to pick his fights where Frankie was concerned and this one wasn't worth getting into. Not now anyway. He was too tired and had other more important issues to address.

Like was she really okay and...*what the heck had she been thinking on the mountain?*

Clenching his jaw against the impulse to yell at her, Nate growled when she stopped at her SUV and dug around in her shoulder bag for her keys. So much for calming his mind, he thought with frustration.

Without looking at him, she asked, "About what?"

"Let's start with you making a target of yourself in a dark parking lot, and ending with driving after being medicated on top of a long shift."

"Don't be ridiculous," she snorted, causing his jaw to harden. "I'm perfectly capable of driving myself. Besides, *all* my shifts are long."

"All the more reason to be careful after taking meds," he snapped, reaching out to snag her shoulder bag. She tried to snatch it back but the move had her sucking in a sharp breath. She abruptly swayed and in the light from the nearby security light he watched her face drain of color.

Cursing, he wrapped an arm around her waist and yanked her roughly against him. The feel of her body, warm and soft against his, had him sucking in his own sharp breath. Putting his hands on her hadn't been part of his plan.

But this pale and terrifyingly fragile woman tugged at something buried so deep he'd forgotten it was there. Something he didn't want to examine too closely.

"C'mon," he muttered wearily. "I'll drive you home."

"I can get myself home, Commander Big Shot," she announced, but her bold statement was ruined when it emerged all slurred and weary. It must have annoyed her because she planted her palms against his chest and shoved. "I'm fine," she grunted, when her efforts failed to move him. "Especially as I've been taking care of myself for a while now, thank you very much."

"That's *Lieutenant* Commander Big Shot," he corrected mildly, allowing her some space but snagging her arm when she tried to stomp off in the opposite direction. He tugged her toward his brand-new four-by-four. "And it's not you I'm worried about, wild thing. It's the other poor saps on the road. Your driving is enough to scare even the most seasoned speedster."

"Hey," she protested, stumbling into a parked car before he could steer her out of the way. "I'm an excellent driver. You should know. You and Jack taught me."

At the mention of Jack, they both seemed to freeze because the last time he'd tried to talk to her about her brother, she'd kind of freaked out. He'd wanted to tell her how much Jack had meant to him—of the promise he'd made to look out for her—but Frankie hadn't wanted to listen. She clearly didn't want to talk now either because her expressive face abruptly closed down.

It had been more than five years and Nate still

missed Jack, especially being back in Port St. John's.

Injecting as much normality and humor into his tone as he could, he said, "That's why I know you suck. Maybe you should get a siren installed." He pulled her upright and was relieved when she allowed him to steer her to the driver's side. "That way people will know to get out of your way. Besides, I'm surprised that piece of junk you drive hasn't fallen apart."

"Hey," she objected again, this time more strongly. "Just because it doesn't fit your lofty idea of perfection it doesn't mean it's ready for the scrap heap, Mr. Everything-is-Better-Newer-and-Shinier. It's just like you to be—"

She stopped abruptly when she realized she wasn't at the passenger side. After a couple of blinks, a slow smile tugged at her full lips and she flashed an upward gaze. For the first time he realized that her smile was wonky and her eyes were a little glazed.

Great. She was as high as a kite.

"You're letting me drive?"

His snort was enough to bring back her scowl. "You're no fun," she accused sulkily, and in the abrupt silence that followed he heard her suck in a sharp breath.

It was the same accusation she'd flung at him the night of her eighteenth birthday. The night she'd pretended to drown in the surf when she'd been an excellent swimmer. The night he'd lost his temper when he'd realized she'd done it to get his attention.

It was also the night he'd realized that a grown-up Frankie—with all the curves of blossoming womanhood—was more dangerous to his mind and body than a whole mountainside of terrorists with their crosshairs on his center mass.

"Get in, Francis," he murmured dryly, disengaging the locks and opening the door. "*I* drive."

"You're still bossy and annoying," she muttered beneath her breath as she gingerly climbed into the cab. "And if I wasn't so tired, I'd tell you that you're not the boss of me."

His lips twisted wryly. "Of course you would. Get in, woman, before my patience runs out and I toss you into the harbor."

She uttered a soft snort and lurched over the gearshift, giving him an eyeful of her curvy bottom. He wanted to look away but he couldn't because, in spite of everything, a grown-up Frankie would tempt a saint.

"I'd like to see you try," she muttered grumpily, and Nate's amusement faded. *None* of this was funny, least of all the sight of her pale, exhausted face. Knowing he was partly to blame made his chest ache.

He pulled himself into the cab and shoved the key in the ignition, studying her out the corner of his eye.

"You okay?"

Her soft snort was accompanied with a dry "Peachy," drawing a long-suffering sigh from Nate. The skinny girl with wild red hair, a smattering of freckles across her nose and a wide contagious smile had turned into a stunning woman.

But the joyful sparkle in her clear green eyes had been replaced by shadows and secrets. Secrets she was keeping from him.

Nate shook his head at himself and started the engine. He shoved the gearstick into reverse and with quick economical moves backed out of the parking and headed for the exit.

At this time of the night it was a quiet drive across town to the little bungalow she called home and he waited until he turned into her driveway before saying, "You ready to talk, Red?"

Out the corner of his eye he saw her go still and it took him a couple of seconds to realize the old nickname he'd given her when she was ten had slipped out without thinking. Maybe it had been the mention of Jack, as though they were still all young, and alive...and together.

Her lush mouth firmed and she turned to face him, gaze unreadable when she'd always been an open book. To him at least.

"About what? I thought we'd settled the issue of me driving in a drug-induced state when I allowed you to shanghai me?"

"It's about your reckless behavior."

"Reckless? Hardly," she snorted, gathering up her shoulder bag and reaching for the door handle. "I was just going to drive home, for God's sake. Not take a joyride through town and along the coast. Besides, I surrendered to your bossy manhandling, didn't I?"

"You know what I'm talking about, Francis," he said wearily. "I'm talking about what you did on the mountain."

"I don't know what your problem is," she half

snarled, lurching upright in her seat as though preparing for a fight. "It's not like I was the one without a safety line. *You* were," she pointed out shortly. "I'm not the one who thinks she's a big, bad indestructible SEAL too cool to die."

"What's that supposed to mean? Of course I'm not indestructible. What gave you that idea?"

"Oh, I don't know," she tossed over her shoulder as she reached again for the door handle and shoved the door open. "Maybe this insatiable need you have to be a damn hero."

She hopped out before he could answer and slammed the door with way more force than necessary before stomping her way up the garden path.

Muttering curses, Nate got out and followed, wondering what he thought he was doing. This was exactly why he needed to keep his distance, because five minutes in her company and he was ready to howl with frustration.

Taking the stairs three at a time, he moved beneath the light to where she was digging in her shoulder bag for her keys. Without looking up, she snarled irritably, "Go away. I'm not in the mood for any of your annoying lectures."

Controlling himself with difficulty, he said mildly, "Humor me," and folded his arms across his chest. Propped against the wall, he studied her pale face in the glow of the overhead porch light. "You owe me that at least."

"Excuse me? I owe *you*?" She gaped up at him for a couple of beats before a scoffing laugh escaped. "I think you have that backward, *Commander Big Shot*," she drawled. "The way *I* remember it, *bub*," she said, poking his abs with a hard finger, "you were on your way over that cliff when *I* saved *you*."

He grabbed her hand before she could drill a hole in his chest, tightening his grip when she tried to snatch it back. Her growl of frustration had his brow arching with amusement.

"Exactly," he said with masculine superiority, knowing it would get a reaction out of her. Besides, why should he be the only one with escalating blood pressure? "You seem to forget how well I know you, Francis," he said quietly. "That daring leap off the ledge was impulsive. You never gave a thought to that safety line and you know it."

"You don't know anything about me, *Nathan*,"

she snapped, and pulled free. "You just *think* you do. You left here when I was a girl to go off to prove what a big badass you were. What's more reckless than that? Besides, I'm not that adoring little kid you once knew, and even if what you say *is* true—and it's not," she snapped, jabbing the air with her keys, "you're lucky I did make that leap, or you'd be whipping poor soldier angels into shape instead of standing here now, annoying me."

It wasn't in the least bit amusing. He sighed. "Frankie—"

"I'm sorry." Her voice hitched. "I wasn't thinking." She was quiet a moment before adding, "I meant you'd be stomping around in hell with your size thirteen boots, trying to save lost souls. Isn't that what you always do, *Lieutenant* Commander? Save lost souls?" She drew in a deep breath as though that brief flash of fire had exhausted her. "I'm not a lost soul," she said flatly, shoving a shaky hand through her hair as she leaned back against the door to study him through drooping lids. "I never was. Only you could never see that."

"Have you forgotten I how many times I saved your skin over the years?" he demanded tersely, recalling how they'd all—he, Jack and Ty—tried to make up for Frankie's parents' disinterest in their daughter, only to have her run circles around them.

She closed her eyes and wearily pushed herself upright, ramming her elbow into his gut when she turned to shove the key into the lock. "I don't need saving, Nate," she muttered. "I can save myself. And even if I did need a savior, it wouldn't be *you*."

Her words burrowed beneath his skin. "I get that," he growled furiously, because that's what she *had* wanted once. "But what you did last night was reckless."

"Don't let it go to your head, stud," she dismissed coolly, pushing the door open before pausing with one foot inside. "I would have done it for anyone. You're just mad because I beat you to it. Mad that the badass Navy SEAL got rescued by a girl."

"Don't make this about me, Frankie," Nate said irritably, ignoring her accusation because what she'd said was ridiculous. Besides, *he* was the trained professional. It was *his* job to save people.

"Why not?" she shot back heatedly. "It's not

like I was alone on that ledge. It's not like I was just going to—" She stopped abruptly and sucked in a sharp breath, turning away.

"It's not like you were just going to what, Frankie?" Nate demanded. "Use your head? Think before you acted? Because that's your usual MO, isn't it? Wade into the fray and damn the consequences?"

The look she sent over her shoulder was filled with hurt and fury. "You know what? Never mind. You brought me home. Thanks." She turned away as though she couldn't bear the sight of him. "You can leave. You're good at that."

He caught her arm. "Excuse me?"

She tried to yank her arm free but he tightened his grip, not wanting her to disappear inside where she'd no doubt continue to ignore him. "If I have to tell you," she drawled smartly, "you're not half as smart as I thought you were."

"And *you*, babe?" he growled. "How smart are *you*?"

She froze, her fiery green eyes turning arctic as she glared up at him. "Tell me you did *not* just call me 'babe'." Her mouth curled in distaste. "Take it back and I might consider letting you live."

It was such a Frankie thing to say that Nate couldn't help the low laugh that escaped him. It was clearly the wrong thing to do because she sucked in a furious breath and punched him.

She tried to punch him again but Nate was expecting it and reacted with lightning-fast reflexes, wrapping his hand around her much smaller fist and yanking her against him.

Dark satisfaction filled him when a shocked squeak emerged from between her parted lips. "You only get one shot, *babe*," he warned silkily, staring into eyes gone dark with surprise.

Infuriated by his warning, by the name he'd used on her when it was what he called all his other women, his laughter—heck, all of the above— Frankie stared up into his hard, handsome face, and with her free hand punched him again. Harder.

Her fist practically bounced off his steel-hard abs and before she could growl her frustration he'd backed her against the wall, both wrists imprisoned in his inescapable grip. She ignored the slight discomfort in her back, furious with the easy way he pinned her hands beside her head.

Her startled protest was interrupted by a low, rough curse that ended on, "You just had to, didn't you?" And then he did something that shocked her even more. He swooped in and slammed his mouth down on hers.

Frankie went utterly still, shock reverberating through her. To be perfectly honest, she'd been hoping to get a reaction from him, but she'd never expected him to…to… *Oh, boy.*

The next instant she thought, *How dare he kiss me?* and tried to bite him, but he broke the kiss, his breathing furious and choppy in the predawn silence. As though he was restraining himself from throttling her. With a great deal of effort.

Yeah, well, she was restraining herself too. From melting into a puddle at his feet. But there was no way she would ever admit it. Even on threat of dismemberment.

"You little hellion," he rasped against her lips, and roughly took her mouth again. This time the kiss lasted longer than those first furious seconds and, completely against her will, Frankie found herself kissing him back. Tentatively at first and then... Wow.

The man certainly knew his way around a woman's mouth. Knew exactly how to use *his* lips to drive her crazy with hard punishing kisses one minute and soft deep caresses the next.

He was warm and solid against her, radiating heat and the kind of strength she needed to keep her knees from wobbling and dumping her at his feet. Was, in fact, keeping her upright with his big hard body.

Someone moaned—she was pretty sure it was her—the sound so breathy and needy she might have cringed if she'd had the capacity to do anything more than respond, feel and...oh, God... make another muffled sound in the back of her throat. Every thought, every protest was stripped away—along with her resistance.

The instant her mouth softened against his, he broke away, drawing back far enough to mutter a string of curses. Even before she managed to fill her lungs, Frankie's first thought was, *What the heck just happened?*

She finally sucked in air and opened her eyes, her body absorbing the hard press and heat of

his, her mind struggling with the fact that he'd…
that he'd…

"Wha—" she croaked, then snapped her mouth
shut before any more embarrassing sounds
emerged and he realized that she was speechless. That the woman who usually had an answer
for everything had been rendered speechless by
a kiss.

By Nate's kiss.

With a low muttered curse, Nate pushed away
from the wall and turned, impatiently thrusting
a hand through his mussed hair as he headed for
the porch stairs.

"Go inside, Frankie," he ordered, his voice low
and intense, sounding unbearably weary.

Feeling her hackles rise at his bossy tone, the
easy way he always seemed to dismiss her, the
way the kiss appeared not to have affected him
when it had practically floored her, all seemed
to crash in on her at once.

"What the hell was that?" she demanded, mortified to discover that her voice shook almost as
much as her knees.

With his back toward her, Nate shoved his
hands in his pockets and sent her a hooded

glance across his shoulder. His face was a study of light and shadows—just like the man himself—and the side of his mouth lit by the porch light twitched at the corner.

"If you don't know," he drawled dryly, "then you're not half as smart I thought you were."

It took a couple of moments for Frankie to realize he'd used her earlier words against her but before she could respond, he had walked away and was pulling open his truck door.

He paused to stare at her across the distance and with a low "Do everyone a favor, Francis. Stay out of trouble," he slid inside and started the engine, leaving Frankie spluttering as his taillights disappeared into the predawn light.

CHAPTER FOUR

FRANKIE HAD BEEN asleep for what felt like mere seconds when she was awakened by banging on her front door. For a moment she thought she'd overslept and jerked upright to stare wide-eyed at her bedside clock.

Twelve fourteen? That couldn't be right, could it? Had her clock stopped during the night?

Her heart pounded a furious drumbeat in her ears and she struggled to remember what day it was. But when her body strongly objected to the sudden move, memory returned in a rush and she sank back into her pillows with a groan.

She'd barely managed to get any sleep, having been awakened several times by confusing dreams that had left her shaking like a leaf one moment and burning up the next. She was tired, achy and needed her sleep or someone was going to pay. Big time.

She carefully found a comfortable spot and was just drifting off when— *Bang, bang, bang.*

"Seriously?" she snarled, throwing back the covers and easing her stiff body off the bed. Her legs felt like cooked noodles and about as useful.

With a muttered curse about the dire consequences to the idiot on her doorstep, she stomped—fine, shuffled—down the stairs, wincing and cursing when every step practically vibrated up her spine into her head.

Sheesh. She felt like she'd rolled down the mountain, hitting every rock on the way or… or spent an entire weekend on a bender. But she was way past the bender stage and no longer did stupid things.

Correction: she *mostly* didn't do stupid things. Last night had been the exception. She'd been so out of it she'd let *him* manhandle her and…and *kiss* her.

She was hugely embarrassed to recall that she hadn't put up much of a fight, especially as there had been some anger and a lot of frustration behind his kiss.

As if he'd wanted her to shut up and kissing her was the only thing he could think of.

Yanking open the door, she squinted up…*way up*…at the huge figure leaning against the wall looking far too rested and relaxed to be the last person she wanted to see. The person responsible for disturbing her sleep. The person who'd left her at four thirty in the morning feeling confused and strangely buzzed.

"Do you know what time it is?" she rasped irritably, carefully lifting an arm and shoving her fingers through her tangled hair. She hoped he hadn't caught the fine tremor in her fingers or the careful way she moved but Nate always saw more than she wanted.

"Had a rough night?" he asked mildly, his mouth—the mouth that had sucked the sass right out of her and the one she'd been dreaming about—twitching when her reply to his asinine observation was to curl her lip in a silent snarl.

Frankie didn't care how she looked. Pausing, she gave a mental eye-roll. Correction. She didn't *want* to care but she'd fallen face first into bed with damp hair and could only imagine how she looked.

"You should be sleeping."

For a few incredulous moments she blinked up

at him as though she hadn't heard him correctly. "Sleeping?" she practically yelped. "I *would* be sleeping, but some idiot is breaking down my door before the sun is even up."

Nate studied her silently from behind his aviator shades before lifting his arm and pointedly looking at a big black navy diving watch. "It's just after noon."

"What are you doing here, Commander?" she demanded huskily. "I told you I don't need a babysitter."

"No, you said you don't need a *keeper*," he corrected. "There's a difference. I happen to disagree but this is being a friend—a *brotherly* friend."

Frankie stilled at his reminder that his interest was fraternal and nothing more. And the guilt that always accompanied the pain when someone mentioned Jack had her retorting, "I have enough friends, and I certainly don't need or want another brother."

For a couple of beats Nate stilled, his jaw flexing as he studied her. And just when she expected him to turn and walk away, he expelled his breath in a half exasperated, half amused whoosh.

"Good thing I know how grumpy you are in

the morning before you've had your caffeine," he drawled dryly, "or your sunny disposition might scare me away." He held out a large to-go mug.

When the aroma of fresh coffee finally hit her brain, Frankie reached out and grabbed it, tempted to forgive him for disturbing her sleep. "I'm only grumpy when I'm trying to sleep and idiots interrupt me. Why are you here again?"

"I brought you breakfast."

"I'm not hungry but thank you for the coffee," she said politely, taking a huge sip and sighing as the hot brew hit her stomach. "Now go away."

Nate chuckled and pushed away from the wall. "She said you'd say that," he said with amused resignation. "Now, either you back up and let me inside or I get ugly because I'd rather face you than an angry Paige."

Frankie narrowed her eyes at him over the top of the to-go cup. "How ugly?"

"I'm trained in close-quarters combat," he said mildly. "How ugly do you *think* it can get?"

The last thing she wanted to be reminded about was his close-quarters combat move from that morning, so she demanded instead, "Why?"

"Why what?"

"Why now?" She took another sip of coffee and felt her head begin to clear. It paid to have her wits about her when dealing with Nate. "You've been home for nine months and not once in all that time did you even pick up the phone and say, 'Hey, how about a drink to catch up on old times?' So I repeat…why now?"

Nate was quiet so long Frankie thought he didn't intend to reply and before she could stop it, hurt lodged like a hard, hot lump in her chest. She stepped back and reached out to close the door before she did or said something she'd regret.

"Never mind," she clipped out frostily. "I can see that you're trying to come up with some lame excuse you think I'm stupid enough to swallow," and was about to close the door when a size thirteen boot stopped her.

Annoyance at his gall edged out the hurt and she put all her weight behind it, trying to force it closed, but all it did was remind her that she'd given the mountain a full-body hug last night.

She grunted. "Move your big clumsy foot before I break it in half."

"Yeah," came his darkly amused voice, "I can't see that happening."

Furious at his masculine display of superiority, Frankie shoved again and nearly whimpered as pain shot up her spine to explode in her skull. She must have made a sound because Nate muttered a few choice curse words.

"Stop before you hurt yourself," he growled. "And before you start yelling at me again, I thought Paige told you to take it easy?"

She curled her lip to snarl at him when long tanned fingers curled around the door and with little visible effort he pushed it open—moving her backward with it.

Only because she didn't want to spill her coffee.

Feeling a little light-headed, she turned and headed for the kitchen before she embarrassed herself by passing out. "Don't let the door hit you on your way out," she snapped over her shoulder, sighing when she heard the door click shut. "Yeah," she muttered. "So much for friendly concern. But thanks for the coffee," she said, then yelped when she turned her head and discovered him right behind her.

"Holy…" she gasped, stumbling into a kitchen cabinet and almost dropping her coffee before managing to set it on the counter with shaking hands. "What the heck are you doing?"

Having nothing to occupy her hands, she folded her arms beneath her breasts and glared at him.

He'd removed his sunglasses and shoved them onto the neck of his white T. "I brought you breakfast and I plan to stay while you eat it." His eyes were sharp and intent as an eagle's and she wished she was wearing more than ancient PJs—wished she'd had more time to dress and put on her mental makeup, because dealing with the adult version of Nate wasn't going to be as simple as dealing with the boy she'd known.

For one thing his eyes were no longer easy to read. No longer the warm honey filled with exasperated affection when he looked at her. It might have annoyed her that she couldn't read him but she got a little sidetracked by the sight of those sexy eyes in the bright light of day.

She knew he'd say they were brown, but not in any stretch of the imagination could such vibrant colors be called something as boring as brown. Brown made her think of mud or tree bark.

His eyes were made up of three distinct colors; honey, amber and onyx. Amber and onyx striations radiated out from the center and a thin onyx circle edged his honey-colored irises, growing or shrinking according to his moods. As a kid she'd been able know what he was thinking but the man had learned to hide his feelings really well.

From the world…or just her?

"I was thinking about the last thing you said to me all those years ago. You said you didn't want to see me again," Nate reminded her mildly, propping his shoulder against the door frame and studying her like she was a particularly interesting bug he'd just discovered.

Shame flooded her at the reminder of the words she'd flung at him that night.

"I was eighteen and a little tipsy," she said defensively, carefully propping her hip against the under-counter cabinet and placing one bare foot on top of the other. "I said a lot of stuff that night I didn't mean and you know it. Besides," she reminded him, "you called me a stupid spoiled brat and told me to grow up. I might have been spoiled and immature but I was *never* stupid."

"Really?" Nate said mildly as he placed a paper

bag on the counter and folded his arms across his wide, hard—she wasn't ogling—chest. "Because I clearly remember you diving off Devil's Point into the sea one night to impress some young punk. That was a really stupid move."

"You, Jack and Ty did it," she pointed out. "Probably hoping you'd get laid by those brainless groupie bimbos you used to date. At least I won a bet."

"You won a broken arm too, but that's not the point. The point is Jack let you run wild just to make up for Frank and Gloria."

"Leave Jack and my parents out of this," she growled, feeling too fragile and exposed beneath those penetrating eyes to think about how inadequate she always felt when people talked about Jack. About how her parents had been so devastated at the death of their golden boy that they'd forgotten that she'd lost her brother too.

She'd tried to be there for them—still tried—but they were always too wrapped up in their grief.

And just like that she was feeling like the worst kind of person because after all this time she was still reacting like a jealous kid.

What kind of person was jealous of a ghost? What kind of person was jealous of a brother she still adored five years after his death? But somewhere in all those mixed-up feelings of jealousy and anger and guilt was the certainty that everyone had set Jack up to die. They'd turned him into someone who'd felt that he should live up to everyone's high expectations by enlisting.

Besides, how better to live up to lofty expectations than dying a hero?

And here in front of her was yet another man who needed to prove himself worthy. Prove he was nothing like his father by becoming—you guessed it—a hero. A man who looked all hot and sexy while doing it. A man who saw her as an annoying little sister he was constantly rescuing from disaster.

Absolutely nothing sexy about that, despite that early-morning kiss.

She mentally rolled her eyes at herself. She really needed to forget that kiss. "Fine. I was spoiled and needed to grow up but I don't do stupid stuff anymore...unless saving you from a two-hundred-foot plunge to death is your idea of stupid." He opened his mouth, probably to say something incredibly manly and insensitive, but Frankie cut him off. "Besides, I don't want to talk about it." Her glare told him that included what had happened earlier that morning. *Ever.*

He shut his mouth on a sigh and just looked at her for a couple of beats before saying quietly, "What happened to you, Francis?"

She didn't pretend to misunderstand. She'd realized after Jack's death that her self-worth wasn't wrapped up in someone else's opinion of her.

But she didn't tell him that. She also didn't know how to handle this quiet, serious Nate either. She shrugged one shoulder. "I grew up like you told me to. If you don't like what you see, Nathan, that's just too bad."

He casually lifted his hand to scratch his jaw but Frankie caught the quick smile he tried to hide. A low sexy chuckle was his only response to her dangerously narrowed gaze. Sexy because those amber bits in his eyes sparkled and sexy because tingles shot from the base of her spine, ending...well, everywhere.

She wanted to find him sexy about as much as she wanted to notice how the stark white cotton T-shirt contrasted with his tanned skin...or the way it stretched over some pretty awesome pecs, abs and biceps, inviting her hands to explore.

She didn't dare. No way.

His darkly amused tone zapped her out of her stupid haze. "Since when do you do what other people say?"

"Since never," she rapped out smartly, embarrassed to be caught having hot thoughts about him while he was laughing at her. "And I told you I didn't want to discuss the past so I'll say this just once—and if you ever bring it up again you're a dead man. You were…right." She practically choked on the word but forced herself to continue. "I needed to— What?" she demanded when he gave a dramatic gasp.

"Did you…did you just say I was right?"

Frankie swung away before she threw the coffee at him. She needed the caffeine fix more than she wanted to hurt him.

"You know what? Never mind. I take it back. You're not right about anything—except maybe the coffee. Which is delicious, by the way." She took another sip to show exactly *how* delicious and moaned with pleasure.

Instantly, Nate's eyes dropped to her mouth

and Frankie experienced that full-body tingle again—like it was possible he was having trouble sticking to his "brotherly" thoughts, no matter what he said. The thought made her knees weak and her head light.

The tense silence was interrupted when she finally caught a whiff of the food on the counter and her stomach decided to announce her hunger by growling…loudly. But she'd already rejected the breakfast and wouldn't be reduced to begging.

At least, not with Nate.

"I just want to be alone with my coffee so we can have our moment," she crooned, licking whipped cream from her lips, which curved in a delighted smile when his eyes instantly darkened. They went all heavy and half-mast and Frankie covered her smile with a yawn. He was definitely thinking non-brotherly thoughts. "But since you're still here, it might be a good time to repeat my question."

Nate's brows drew together over the bridge of his nose but his gaze was slow to return to hers. Probably with as much frustration as bafflement because, God knew, she had that kind of effect on men.

"Which question was that?"

"Why are you here, Commander?"

"I brought you breakfast and before you say you're not hungry, I heard your stomach growling. So don't think about spiting yourself just because I brought it. Besides, I bet you haven't considered that your body needs to recover."

"I *was* recovering," she reminded him. "But you interrupted my beauty sleep."

His eyes gleamed with amusement as he took in her wild red-gold hair, ancient T-shirt and soft, faded flannel PJ pants, and for the first time in her life Frankie wished she was wearing something sexy. Not because she wanted him to find her sexy but to prove to him that she was all grown up.

Okay and maybe just a little part of her wanted him to eat his heart out because she was no longer that brash, skinny, underdeveloped teenager jealous of all the attention he gave other girls.

"Don't say it," she warned.

"Say what?"

"That I need all the beauty sleep I can get."

He gave a low sexy chuckle that did annoying things to her belly. To convince herself it was just hunger pangs, she reached out and grabbed the paper bag from Sid's, a popular diner on the boardwalk, and drew it against her as though she was afraid he'd steal it. When she opened it and peered inside, she nearly swooned at the delicious aromas escaping. And if she wasn't mistaken, he'd brought her favorite breakfast. But then again Paige had probably told him.

There were two containers in the bag, one much smaller than the other. She focused her attention on the larger container because she knew what was inside.

"I thought you said you weren't hungry."

"I'm not," she lied, opening the container and practically salivating at what she uncovered. "But Sid's harvest eggs Benedict are the best in Washington. Team that with crispy bacon and mushrooms and I could almost forgive you for disturbing my beauty sleep. Besides, I figure if I eat something you'll leave and I can go back to bed."

"You're a terrible liar, Francis," Nate said mildly. "Always were." He was quiet a moment before saying softly, "I'm glad to see some things haven't changed."

Not wanting to discuss changes, Frankie reached out to open the cutlery drawer and sucked in a sharp breath when the move reminded her that she'd tried to be a superhero last night.

"Looks like your stubborn streak is bigger than ever," Nate said dryly, and opened the drawer.

"Hey." She grabbed the fork he held out and jabbed it in the air. "I can fight my own demons, thank you very much. This morning I wrestled quite a few of my own—" Realizing what she was about to admit, Frankie shoveled a huge forkful into her mouth and prayed he didn't notice her almost-confession.

"Having nightmares?"

"Don't be ridiculous!" she dismissed, shoveling a piece of bacon into her mouth. But when Nate just looked at her she added casually, "Nothing a girls' night out won't cure." Or a hot and heavy bout of sex. But that was about as likely as winning the lottery.

"What?" she asked warily, quickly backing up when she realized that Nate had moved closer. He reached out and cupped her chin in his big warm hand, tightening his grip when she tried to jerk away.

"What?" she demanded, a little spooked by the abrupt intensity in his gaze.

"You had nightmares? About this morning?"

"Well, the kiss wasn't *that* bad," she tried to joke, but he just continued to hold her gaze until she was afraid he could see all the way to her soul. "Fine, yes," she sighed, shoving his hand away and stepping out of reach. "I had a few nightmares. Big deal."

"About? I'm only asking," he continued when she rolled her eyes, "because it's better to talk them through. Keeps the dreams from becoming real inside your mind."

"Oh, please," she snorted dryly. "Now you sound like a shrink." No way was she talking about her dreams or nightmares. Especially not to him. Mostly because they'd been about him. About the fact that he'd slipped from her reach and disappeared into a stygian abyss.

"Is that what the Navy shrinks make you do?" she asked, to cover the fact that just thinking about him dying had left her with a hollow feeling of devastation. "Talk about your dreams?"

"Among other things," he murmured, and Frankie tried not to feel disappointed when his expression shut down and he drew away. Shutting her out. "But the other reason I'm here is to say thank you."

"For?"

His mouth twisted wryly. "For that stupid leap off the ledge."

"Stupid?" she demanded. "Is that what you call saving your dumb hide?"

"That's not what I meant," he said quietly. "I meant if you hadn't been attached to the safety line you would have gone over with me."

She rolled her eyes and shrugged. "I was attached, so what's the big deal? You think I should have just let you go over?"

"No, that's not—"

"Well, let me tell you something, Com-man-der." She jabbed her fork in the air with each syllable. "Maybe you've forgotten how things work around here. We look out for each other, we catch each other when we fall, we—"

"Thank you."

Frankie was silent a moment as anger and frustration drained away, leaving her exhausted.

"You're welcome," she said quietly, and sucked in a shaky breath. "Now, if that's all, I'm tired. I didn't get much sleep."

"Have you taken your medication?"

Frankie frowned and looked around the kitchen, trying to remember what she'd done with the prescription Paige had given her. "I went straight to bed… I haven't got it filled yet. I'll do it later," she said, trailing him when he turned and disappeared out of the kitchen. She found him in the hallway, emptying her purse onto the entrance table.

She rushed forward to stop him. "Hey! That's my purse. What do you think you're doing?"

He found what he was looking for and with her prescription in hand opened the front door and stepped onto the porch. "I'll see you get this," he said, and trotted down the stairs, heading for his shiny new toy.

"You're not the boss of me, Commander Big Shot," she yelled at his retreating back, furious that she allowed him to get under her skin. Why couldn't she behave like the sophisticated professional she was? "And next time don't expect me to save you. In fact, next time I'll help you off a ledge myself."

* * *

Nate couldn't stop the sigh or the wry grin that tugged at the corner of his mouth because dealing with Frankie was always like handling primed explosives.

Folding her prescription, he thrust it into his pocket and slid his aviators over his eyes. After the storm of yesterday, the sky was a clear cerulean blue so bright and clean that it hurt just to look at it.

During the past ten years he'd lost count of the times he'd dreamed of Washington skies after a wild storm. In the hot, dry climes of the Middle East, where every breath seemed to suck the moisture right out of you, he'd often found himself missing the cool humidity of his home town as much as he'd missed the people and his family. Missed Frankie.

But if he'd missed Frankie Bryce, it was because she'd been like a kid sister, he told himself. He'd grown up looking out for her, saving her from herself, and now that Jack was gone, Nate was left with a promise that weighed heavily on his shoulders.

Pulling open the driver's door, Nate looked

across the roof of his truck at the wild woman glaring at him from her porch and sighed. He could feel the waves of irritation and frustration reaching across to him.

"Get some sleep, Francis," he said, knowing the name would irritate her. "You look like hell."

And before she could fling any more insults his way, Nate slid into the driver's seat, started the engine and shoved the truck into gear.

Besides, irritation was better than the cool indifference she'd treated him to since his return, even if he'd deserved it. It meant the old Frankie was still in there somewhere. The Frankie he hadn't realized he'd missed until he'd seen her again and discovered a poised, aloof woman with cool green eyes and a soft unsmiling mouth. A woman he didn't know quite how to deal with because she was nothing like the vibrant, feisty young girl he'd known.

That young girl he'd had no problem treating like a kid sister. The woman she'd become…well, not so much.

Besides, he had a debt to pay Jack and his family. They'd been there when Tom Oliver, Nate's father, had skipped town, leaving a devastated family to cope with a one-hundred-thousand-dollar debt on a high-school teacher's salary. They'd given an overwhelmed kid a place where he could be himself, had treated him as one of the family and showered him with the same love and attention they'd given to their son.

Love and affection they should have shown their daughter—but hadn't. Maybe Frankie's dad hadn't known what to do with a wild little girl, but he'd had no problem stepping in as the father figure Nate had needed, teaching him alongside his own son how to be a man—how to catch a ball, how to bait a hook and pilot a fishing trawler. Stuff his own father hadn't stuck around for.

Maybe it was guilt about that—or the fact that Jack was gone and it felt wrong somehow to think of Frankie as a woman—that had kept him away from her.

Besides, what did he have to offer a woman, anyway? He had too many responsibilities as it was, helping his mother pay off the huge debt his father had left behind, and helping take care of Terri.

In the past he'd felt suffocated by all the responsibility. It was the reason he'd left Port St. John's in the first place. To live his own life, get a couple of degrees and still be able to take care of his family. It was what a man was supposed to do. Not bail at the first sign of hard times.

Nate had always been determined to prove to everyone that he wasn't his father. Prove that he wasn't a womanizer who shirked his responsibilities or deliberately broke promises. And if that meant he'd have to avoid one feisty redhead... then that was exactly what he would do.

CHAPTER FIVE

EVEN THOUGH IT had been nearly twenty-four hours since he'd returned to Frankie's and dropped off her medicine, Nate still found his mind wandering back to her and to *that* kiss.

The only thing that was going to distract him was focusing on the other, less frustrating, women in his life so he offered to take his sister to her physical therapy session on his day off.

Terri had been as wild as Frankie and the inactivity of being a paraplegic drove her insane. She was doing an online degree in conservation because she wanted to be a forest ranger. If anyone could overcome a spinal injury, it was his sister.

After the grueling session that left her covered in sweat and snarling like a caged leopard, Nate steered them toward the Gelato Grotto on the boardwalk, hoping to put her in a better mood. But Terri knew exactly what he was doing.

"You know that I'm not a kid anymore, don't

you?" she drawled dryly, after they'd left the shop with their purchases and headed for the harbor. The picturesque walkway was always filled with tourists and gave them a clear view of the strait. It was a sight Nate had missed more than he'd thought he would and it never failed to put his sister in a better mood. "Because ice cream doesn't fix a broken back."

"According to Paige, it fixes everything," he said absently, performing a few wheelies with her wheelchair and feeling his heart lift when she laughed. "Besides, I'm really enjoying your sunny disposition and was hoping to spend a pleasant afternoon in your company."

"Liar," she snorted, not in the least offended by his sarcasm. "You can't schmooze me like all your women, Nate. I'm too smart and I know you too well. You're giving Mom a break."

"Of course I am…and I'm spending time with my best girl."

Terri nearly snorted ice cream out of her nose. "If that's true then you need to get laid," she observed smartly. "Clearly you need more excitement in your life."

"I have enough excitement, thanks," Nate

sighed, thinking of the confrontations he'd had with Frankie the last few times their paths had crossed. He knew it was mostly his fault but the woman was ornery enough to put a badger to shame.

Terri made a mocking sound in her throat. "That's for sure."

Nate frowned down at her in a way that usually made strong men pause. "What's that supposed to mean?" But she ignored his look and licked a dollop of ice cream.

"It's all over social media, you know."

That wasn't an answer that Nate had expected. "What is?" he demanded curiously.

Terri made a scoffing sound. "Oh, come now, Commander Coastie. Surely you've seen it? The man with all the advanced engineering degrees?"

Nate stared at her in confusion, wondering if she was on a sugar overload.

She rolled her eyes. "One of which is in computers?"

"What are you talking about?"

"Yeesh," she huffed out impatiently. "I'm talking about last night, dummy."

At the mention of last night Nate froze, his mind

instantly going back to that kiss on Frankie's porch in the early hours. Had someone seen them? Was his biggest mistake since coming home out there for everyone to see?

Frankie was going to kill him.

But showing any kind of weakness to his sister would be like putting out a welcoming mat for an invading army of Huns.

Instead he asked casually, "Last night?"

"Frankly, I think you should tell Mom before someone else does," she said shortly. "Before she freaks out."

Freaks out? Nate thought, feeling a little insulted on Frankie's behalf. He'd thought his mother liked Frankie. She was always talking about her. Francis this, Francis that. Now she was going to freak out because he'd kissed her?

Or maybe she'd be mad Nate had taken advantage of an old family friend.

"Just because I kissed Frankie doesn't mean—" She made a choking sound and he whipped her around, cursing when he saw her expression. "We are talking about that, aren't we?"

His sister was smirking as though she'd just tricked him into revealing state secrets. "You kissed Frankie?" She appeared delighted—and more than a little gleeful. "Well, it's about time."

"No, it's not," he said curtly. "Frankie's like a sister to me, you know that. Besides, she's nuttier than Mom's fruitcake."

Terri's expression was a mix of disgust and pity. "You're an idiot. Frankie's fun, not crazy. But in the spirit of full disclosure I'm talking about the way the woman-who's-like-a-sister dived off that ledge to save you."

"What?"

Terri rolled her eyes. "Oh, puh-*leez*. I'm talking about the fact that you nearly died last night and I had to learn about it online in a video shot by one of the guys on the chopper." She reached out to poke him. "I'm talking about Frankie saving your ass and nearly dying too… And all you can say is—" her voice dropped an octave "'—she's like a sister to me.' Are you insane?"

Nate shoved impatient fingers through his hair. "She was injured saving my ass, as you so elegantly put it, and I… I lost my head a little."

Terri paused with a frown. "She's okay, isn't she?"

Nate sighed and said more gently, "Of course

she's okay. You know Frankie. She's like a cat with multiple lives."

"Nine lives, you mean."

He snorted. "She used up fifteen lives before she was ten."

"Well, she isn't a kid anymore," Terri pointed out unnecessarily. As if he could forget that after last night…and this morning. "I think you should buy her a ton of ice cream to say thank you."

"I took her breakfast."

"How about dinner and dancing…or maybe a sail along the coast with a picnic lunch? She'd like that."

Nate sent her a sideways frown. "Are you by any chance matchmaking, miss nosy?"

Her snort told him exactly what she thought about his suggestion. "Heck, no," she told him. "You're the last person I'd sic on Frankie. I *like* her."

He blew out an exasperated breath. "Why, what's wrong with me?"

She arched her brow and laughed. "Other than you have a hero complex and she hates heroes? A lot, believe me."

That surprised him. "She hates heroes?" He

shook his head as if to clear it because Frankie was always trying to show she was the bravest and the most daring. "You know… Never mind. Why is this even relevant?"

Her expression became unreadable. "It isn't, I'm just saying." She shrugged. "I lived with you for thirteen years before you went off to become a hero. And for six months when you came back. I'm glad you moved into your own place. You're annoying. You eat all the good stuff, hog the remote and leave wet towels all over the place."

"No, that's you."

"Oh, yeah." She grinned and licked her cone. "My bad. So. Wanna see it?"

"See what?"

She gave a huge eye-roll that suggested he was a moron and pulled out her phone. "The video. It's pretty awesome now that I know you're safe."

While she was accessing whatever site she was looking for, Nate threw the last of his cone in the trash. He was wiping his hands when his phone rang.

"Hey, Paige, how's things?"

"Did you hear? Have you seen her?" She sounded out of breath.

He frowned at the odd note of anxiety in her voice. "Hear what? And if you're talking about your best friend, yes, I did. I took her breakfast, which she ate because I waited. Just as you ordered."

"That's great," Paige said impatiently. "But not what I'm talking about."

"What *are* you—"

"A call's just come in. There's been a fire and Fr—"

His blood went cold. "I'll be right there." He was already on the move when he remembered Terri. He grabbed her wheelchair and began speeding along the boardwalk. "I've got to get you home."

"What's wrong? Is something wrong with Frankie?"

"Yes. No... I don't know," he said, battling frustration, irritation and outright terror. "Paige just said something about a fire."

"A fire? Well, go, you idiot," she yelled, slapping at his hands on the wheelchair handles. "I can take care of myself."

"No—"

"I can get to the rehab center myself, Nate." She

paused and then with extreme reluctance promised, "I'll call Mom, I promise."

After wrestling with his conscience for a couple of beats, Nate caved. "All right. But don't do anything stupid and don't talk to charming strangers."

"Yeah, yeah, I know," Terri said impatiently. "Go." She held up her phone. "See? Already calling Mom."

Nate paused only a moment before taking off. He didn't trust his sister to call their mom so he put Ty on speed dial the instant he got back to his truck.

"I heard," Ty said the moment he picked up. "Is she okay?"

"Terri's fine but I wonder—"

"I was talking about Frankie. Did something happen to Terri?"

"No, I was just— Never mind." He shook his head to clear it of the panic that had taken root. "Can you pick her up? Terri, I mean. I took her for ice cream and a walk on the boardwalk after her therapy session and—"

"Already on my way," Ty interrupted, and Nate could hear the sound of keys and the slam of a door. "Get to our girl. I hear she got there before the fire guys and had to go in."

"Got there? Got where?" He gripped the steering wheel until his knuckles turned white. "I thought— Look, never mind. I'm nearly at her house."

"Let me know how—"

"I will," Nate said, and disconnected before he had an accident because he was taking corners on two wheels.

Fortunately, it was the middle of the afternoon and the roads were relatively quiet. He made good time getting from the harbor to Frankie's neighborhood and took a moment to thank the government for the advanced driver training he'd received as part of SEAL training.

As it was, all he really had to do was follow the signs of destruction. Or in this case the sound of sirens and the cloud of black smoke rising into the air.

That was Frankie, he thought with his heart in his throat. Always needing to show that she was ready to wade into the fray at a moment's notice. His gut clenching, Nate gunned the engine, barely missing taking out a couple of trash cans left on the curb.

His dread eased only slightly when he arrived at the scene and discovered her house still intact. Emergency vehicles blocked the road and a crowd had gathered but it seemed like all the excitement was over because a couple of firemen were already rolling up their hoses.

He didn't see Frankie anywhere.

Nate parked his truck and headed toward a couple of EMTs. He had to push his way through the onlookers and caught snippets of conversation as he went.

"It's a good thing she was home… I've never seen anything like it… She just waded into all that smoke and flames… I'd just put the baby down when I heard yelling… It was an age before she emerged with Mrs. Wallace… I couldn't believe my eyes. It was like something from a movie… Barely stopped before running right back inside for Mr. Wallace… I heard the EMTs say she suffered burns along with smoke inhalation…"

Nate sucked in a sharp breath and his heart clenched in his chest. Even if they hadn't mentioned her name, he knew they were talking about Frankie. All he could think of were the words *she suffered burns*.

Cursing himself for not keeping a closer eye on her, Nate approached the EMTs, only to find that Frankie had already been taken to the medical center, homeowner Mr. Wallace was in a bad way, and the worst of the damage was in the back of the house. The latter they'd told him in low voices because Mrs. Wallace was being prepped a short distance away for transport to the ER and they didn't want her to hear.

Nate thanked them and ran back to his truck, breaking the speed limit in his haste to get to the hospital. Offensive driving was one thing when you were dodging bullets and IEDs but another thing entirely when you were negotiating suburban residential streets.

He found parking and headed straight for the ER.

"Francis Bryce," he began, pausing when the duty nurse's eyes widened and her mouth dropped open.

"Omigosh, it's…it's… Nancy, it's *him*," she squeaked, as though Nate wasn't standing right in front of her. "Come quickly…it's him. The…the *guy*."

Nate felt his forehead tighten.

"I'm sure you have me confused with someone else," he began, only to be interrupted.

"Oh, no," the nurse said emphatically. "I'm pretty sure you're the one Frankie saved last night." Ignoring the reference to the previous night, Nate continued, "I heard she was brought in. Can I see her?"

"Oh…uh… I'm not sure—"

"Of course you can see her," Nancy announced with a bright smile. "She's in Room Three."

Nate thanked her and headed through the swing doors separating the waiting area from the examination rooms, and nearly ploughed into the small figure emerging. Paige Carlyle uttered a startled squeak and backed into the trolley beside the door. She would have gone flying if he hadn't shot out a hand and caught her.

"Hey, careful there, Dr. P."

"Nate? Oh, thank God you're here." Tears pooled in her large hazel eyes, turning his heart to mush and making his gut clench.

Man, he hated it when women cried. "What's wrong? Is it bad? How is she?"

She sucked in a deep breath and blinked rapidly a few times until her eyes cleared. "Well…" She gave a ragged laugh. "I swear when people say she has nine lives they aren't kidding but—"

Unable to wait any longer, Nate gently nudged her aside and shoved open the door, coming to an abrupt halt when he found Frankie sitting on the bed, covered in soot, her hair standing out around her blackened face like she'd stuck her finger into a socket.

An oxygen mask covered her nose and mouth and the only color in her face was the startling green of her eyes. They were red-rimmed and a little glazed.

She looked as though she'd been pulled out through a chimney—backward. But at least she was breathing. Well, sort of, he amended when she broke off sucking in clean air to hack up half a lung.

The ER nurse finished setting up a drip and sent her a concerned look. "Take it easy, Frankie."

Nate swept his gaze quickly over Frankie to check for injuries and when he got to her feet, which were wrapped in blood-soaked bandages, he sucked in a sharp breath.

The next instant he was abruptly sucked back into a time and place that had no bearing on the here and now; a place filled with the acrid smell of burning, mingled with dust and blood, sounds of the dying slowly filling his ringing ears.

As though she knew, Paige touched his arm, yanking him back to the present so fast his head spun and his gut heaved.

Every muscle in his body tightened.

"Don't freak out," she murmured, briskly rubbing his back. "It looks a lot worse than it is. She cut her feet on some broken glass, that's all."

The back of Nate's skull tightened as he struggled to keep from being sucked right back into the battle that had taken the lives of two of his crew and left another an amputee.

"What the hell, Frankie?" he demanded hoarsely, bringing up both hands to rub his palms over his face, hoping no one had caught that flashback. Hoping no one saw the fine tremor in his fingers or the fact that he wanted to march over there and yank her into his arms—prove that she really was okay.

Her reply was to roll her eyes and give a disgusted snort as though he was an idiot, and the impulse changed to wanting to shake her for scaring the life out of him.

"Of course I'm fine," she croaked hoarsely. "A little singed, that's all." She coughed again and tried to hide a wince, but Nate wasn't fooled in the least. She was hurting from last night or this afternoon or both.

"Singed? Is that why you're running around in your underwear?"

"My pajama pants caught fire so I ditched them."

His ears rang. "You're kidding, right?"

"Smoldering," she rasped quickly, at what she probably saw in his face. "They were smoldering, that's all."

"Don't try to talk," the ER nurse ordered sternly, sending Nate a warning frown.

"Keep breathing that air, Frankie," Paige said quickly. "And, Nate, if you're going to upset her, Kendra is going to insist you leave."

"Me? I upset *her*?" He thrust a hand through his hair, wondering absently if his fingers really were shaking. "I think you have that wrong,

Doc." He marched up to the bed and gently took Frankie's chin in his hand, looking her over. He noticed the reddened patches of skin along her arms and legs.

"Your hair looks like it got stuck in a fire tornado," he growled, lifting a hand to feel the frizzled ends.

"Hey," she croaked, lethargically slapping his hand away. "Who asked you for fashion advice?"

"Some fashion," he muttered, and the nurse sent him a look that almost vaporized *his* hair.

"It's nothing a little visit to the salon won't fix," she soothed cheerfully. "In fact, Jasmine will have you looking like a cover model in no time." She glared a warning at Nate. "No time at all. In the meantime, I'll go check on my other patient. Dr. Carlyle, I need some advice about the woman in Room Four."

In the abrupt silence that followed their departure Nate heard Frankie's labored breaths and struggled to control his emotions. It ratcheted up his annoyance a couple thousand notches because he felt responsible.

"I leave you for a couple of hours and look what

happens," he clipped out. "You go charging into a burning house. Do you have a death wish?"

The look she sent him suggested he had the IQ of a rock. "That's a stupid thing to say."

"Is it?"

"Of course it is," she rasped irritably. "I'm not the one who left home to go fight terrorists and get blown up," she pointed out. "Besides, I only did what anyone else would have done."

"Are you sure about that?"

She frowned and ignored the question. "I've known the Wallaces all my life, Nate. I couldn't just leave them in there." She took a moment to suck in a careful breath, before demanding on a wheezy sob that reached into his chest and ruthlessly squeezed his heart, "Have you seen what fire does to people?"

He had. A buddy in the teams had died when his chopper had crashed and burst into flames. The remains hadn't even looked human.

Frankie didn't wait for his answer. "Can you…?" she rasped before taking a few gasps of oxygen. "Can you check on Mr. Wallace for me? He…he was unconscious when I found him and Paige won't tell me anything." She stopped abruptly when she realized that Nate wasn't responding. Quick tears filled her eyes and she turned away. "Oh, God. He didn't make it, did he? I was too late." Her shoulders slumped and she lifted a hand to cover her eyes. "I called and called...but I... I couldn't find him." She swallowed hard and devastated him when a lone tear slid out from under her concealing hand. "And it...it reminded me...of...of—"

"Frankie," he rasped, reaching out to gently cradle her trembling hand in his. Her tears and pain made him feel helpless and angry because he didn't know how to deal with them. Besides, he knew she was thinking about Jack...that he'd died thousands of miles from home—in hostile territory—far from anyone who cared about him.

"I haven't heard anything about Mr. Wallace. Don't jump to conclusions, okay?" he urged, fighting the urge to pull her close and wondering when Paige would return. Women were much better at this kind of stuff. Men bumbled their way through, so terrified of saying the wrong thing that they invariably did.

Frankie was always so strong and feisty that

seeing her looking fragile and battling tears alarmed him.

He gave her hand a gentle squeeze before retreating a couple of steps, shoving his hands into his pockets, feeling clumsy and inadequate. It was a new and very unwelcome feeling.

"By the time I got to the house you were already gone," he admitted gruffly. "I came straight here."

"You didn't have to, you know," she rasped kind of fiercely. "I'm fine." Then ruined her declaration by hacking up the other lung.

"You will be."

She sent him a suspicious look from red-rimmed eyes. "What's that supposed to mean?"

"It means," he said, pulling out his cellphone, "that I'm going to ensure you are."

"I'm a big girl, Nathan. I've been taking care of myself for a long time."

"Tonight you don't have to, unless the doctors are going to admit you."

"For what?"

"A psych evaluation would be a great start."

"Ha-ha. Funny. But you needn't concern yourself. Paige has already offered to babysit me."

"Paige? Seriously? You're willing to be the third wheel with the two lovebirds?"

"Hey!" Paige protested, appearing at the door. "I'll have you know—"

"That Ty would be happy with the arrangement?"

"Of course he will," she said firmly. "He loves Frankie."

"Not after a couple of days, he won't," Nate replied mildly.

"Hey!" This time it was Frankie who objected. "I can hear you and I don't need a babysitter. I promise to go home, get into bed and sleep for a week." Nate slid a sideways look at Paige, who was trying not to laugh and ended up rolling her eyes instead.

"What?" Frankie demanded.

"Nothing," Paige said innocently, and before Frankie could demand an answer, Dr. Luther entered the room.

"Okay, young lady," the older man said briskly. "Let's get you checked out." He fitted his stethoscope into his ears. "Dr. Carlyle, if you're not busy perhaps you could ask Nancy at the desk if she can scare up some spare scrubs. Our girl has given the town enough to talk about without wandering around in a hospital gown."

Nate sent Frankie a hooded glance and allowed Paige to nudge him out of the room. Besides, now that he'd seen she was okay, he needed a few moments to himself. Remind himself that she was okay.

"You okay?" Paige asked quietly, as though reading his mind. "Because Frankie is going to be. Okay, I mean," she babbled, rubbing his arm like he needed comforting. "She's a fast healer and—"

Nate shoved a hand through his hair and gave a ragged laugh that felt as though it had been torn from him. "Are you trying to convince me or yourself?"

"Well..." She expelled her breath in a loud whoosh. "Maybe a little of both. But she's not reckless, Nate, she's not irresponsible. Okay, so I maybe I overheard you talking," she admitted a little sheepishly when he arched a brow. "She'd never admit it but I think she feels guilty for being alive when—"

"When Jack's dead."

"Yes," she agreed quietly, looking upset. "I

don't know her parents very well, but I think they make her feel that she should have been the one…to, well—"

"They don't mean it," Nate interrupted, knowing full well that they might not mean it but they had always tended to behave as if Frankie was somehow less important than Jack. His friend had always felt guilty about what was sometimes obvious to others and had tried his best to protect Frankie from it. He hadn't always succeeded. "I've seen many parents of soldiers that are KIA react in the same way. A bit of anger, guilt and what-ifs."

"And you, Nate? Are you suffering survivor's guilt?"

"We all have ghosts that haunt us, Paige," he murmured, and headed for the exit to call Ty. Most civilians had no idea what young men were expected to do in defense of their country, things that changed them and left indelible scars, both inside and out.

He had them too and had mostly learned to deal with them. But every so often something happened and he was flung back in time. These days he didn't have as many flashbacks, but early this morning when he'd finally slept he'd had a doozy of a nightmare, like the ones that used to plague him.

And then that flashback in the ER. He'd learnt years ago that there was little use in dwelling on things he couldn't control. Maybe Frankie was one of those things but she was just going to have to learn that his will was stronger than hers.

CHAPTER SIX

WOOZY FROM ALL the pain meds, Frankie not-so-meekly acquiesced to the wheelchair ride and then the indignity of being carried to Nate's truck. She might have been impressed by his strength if she hadn't been offended by his high-handedness, by the ease with which he'd swept her into his arms like Rhett Butler—all while ignoring her protests—if it hadn't annoyed the heck out of her.

Oh, yeah. And the way she reeked of *eau de* smoke when he smelled awesome—like fresh sea air and warm, sexy man.

Sheesh. Why was it that when a girl really needed to look *out-of-his-league* stunning, she ended up looking and smelling like smoldering roadkill—or like she'd been mudwrestling?

If it had been any other man—or if she'd been able to saunter out of the hospital under her own steam—Frankie might not have cared, but it was the man who'd been her first crush, the man who'd then crushed her. The man who now had the indecency to look like the hottest contender for sexiest man alive.

"You know my mother's more than happy to have you stay with her for a couple of days," Nate said, once he turned onto the highway.

"I love your mom, Nate, but she has more than enough to do without running after me. And Terri is exhausting," she admitted with a raspy chuckle. "Even in a wheelchair she has more energy than the rest of us put together." She yawned. "Besides, Paige said she'd come around after her shift."

Nate said nothing and Frankie finally turned her head to study his profile. It was the profile of a man who'd learnt to hide his thoughts and emotions well, a man who'd probably seen and done things in the past fifteen years that she couldn't begin to imagine.

He was no longer the boy who'd grown up trying to live down his father's reputation by taking on more responsibility than his thin shoulders could carry. And while his shoulders were now wide and heavy with muscles, he'd proved time and again that he could be counted on.

She remembered overhearing people talk about Tom Oliver and wondering how his wife put up with his womanizing ways. She hadn't understood what that had meant at the time, but if he'd looked anything like Nate, she could totally understand women finding the man irresistible.

She remembered how much Nate had hated being compared to his father and wondered if he still did or if he'd realized he was his own man. Besides, he was hard, rugged and intense— way hotter and more irresistible than any shallow pretty boy looking for a good time. He was a man a woman could count on when the going got tough. He was...

"What?"

She blinked when she realized he'd caught her staring. "Huh?"

"You're staring like you're waiting for me to morph into a mutant."

"Actually," she rasped, "I was hoping for Ryan Reynolds but no amount of squinting is helping."

A wry smile twisted his mouth. "Well, it's good to see your sense of humor remains unscathed."

"A little singed around the edges maybe, but

gimme a couple days and I'll be a regular comedy act."

"Is that what you think people expect from you, Francis?"

She scoffed, "Well, not with a name like that."

"What's wrong with Francis?"

She grimaced and admitted with a raspy cough, "It sounds like I was conceived in a church and, let's face it, it's kind of girly."

He arched a brow. "I don't see the problem."

"Are you calling me a girly girl?" she demanded, unsure if she should be insulted or not.

Nate chuckled and turned away. "After living with women most of my life," he drawled, "I've discovered that answering a question like that is the same as wading through a muddy minefield. Explosions will happen, no matter what I say." He took a corner and accelerated up a quiet residential street where televisions flickered in lighted windows. "Let's talk about today instead, shall we."

Frankie immediately turned away because she knew what was coming. He'd accuse her of being reckless and not thinking about how her actions affected other people. Only thing was, she *had* been thinking about how her actions would affect others.

The Wallaces.

"Let's not," she whispered, because her throat hurt. "Let's just agree to disagree. Just this once…until I get my zing back. Then you can lecture me all you want."

Nate fell silent, giving Frankie the opportunity to study him out the corner of her eye. His mouth was a firm, uncompromising line that reminded her of their kiss. But that was about as dangerous as leaping off a ledge without a safety line. Finally, he flicked her a sideways look and sighed, which drew a dry "Look at us, all adult and mature," from her.

"Well, one of us anyway."

Frankie wanted to roll her eyes but she yawned instead. "I know that was an insult but I'm going to ignore it. You can just drop me off. I can take it from here."

Nate continued to say a whole lot of nothing, which suited her just fine. She wasn't in the mood to talk either and when he turned into her driveway she couldn't stop a shudder from forming at the sight of the blackened evidence of the fire that might so easily have taken her elderly neighbors.

Even now Vince Wallace was in a coma and Thelma fighting for every breath. Tears pricked the backs of her eyes and, rather than cry in front of Nate, Frankie gathered up her bag of medical supplies and hopped out almost before the truck had come to a stop. The instant her foot made contact with the ground she was reminded of the glass she'd walked over.

She yelped silently, turning away to hide a pained grimace. *Great.* Even her exits lacked zing.

"Thanks," she rasped, before beginning to hobble up the path. The next thing she knew Nate was sweeping her off her feet and muttering something about her stubbornness.

Too weary to protest, she laid her head against his shoulder and let him carry her up the stairs.

She opened her mouth to say, *Thank you, I can take it from here*, but he ignored her, shoving open her door and heading up the stairs. Instead of taking her to the master bedroom, he made a beeline for the bathroom.

Frankie scowled at him, even though she'd also

planned to make it her first stop. "Dr. Luther said I shouldn't shower."

"Yeah, and we all know you'll ignore his advice, so Paige gave me instructions on how to re-apply your dressings," he clipped out, depositing her on the side of the bath as though he couldn't wait to get rid of her.

"Look," she huffed out irritably. "If I need help, I'll call Paige." Which was a total lie. No way was she bothering anyone with something as simple as showering.

"It's no bother," he said mildly, his sideways glance casual and more than a little amused as he reached into the shower stall and turned on the water. As though he knew she was lying to get rid of him.

It was the amusement that finally got to her. She stood and shoved him out the door. "Go. Away."

He took a couple of beats to study her before snagging the bag of medical supplies out of her bandaged hands. He nodded at the shower. "Call if you need anything."

Her answer was to slam the door and then curse the fact that there hadn't been a lock on it for about twenty-five years. Not since she'd locked herself in the bathroom when she was five and her grandfather had had to take the door off its hinges to get her out.

Frankie felt tears prick her eyes and ruthlessly suppressed them. She wasn't crying because she missed Nanna and Gramps and she wasn't crying because Nate had left without a fight. She was… she was…*well*, a girl didn't need to have a reason.

Especially when her life was unraveling faster than ribbon at Christmas. Maybe…maybe she was just emotional because of the stress of the past twenty-four hours.

But Frankie knew it wasn't that. Her throat hurt, her back hurt from last night's scrapes and bruises and now, along with random patches of blistered skin, her hair looked like she'd crawled through the furnaces of hell.

She was a mess.

Her life was a mess.

And now…and now she'd chased away the last person alive that she really trusted.

More tired and miserable than she'd ever been in her life, Frankie stripped out of the borrowed scrubs and stepped into the shower.

The hot water hit her abused flesh and she quickly adjusted the heat to accommodate her scorched skin. After a minute, she planted her blistered palms flat against the tiles, closed her eyes and let the water wash away the soot and the memories of the past two days.

She hadn't realized she was crying until she heard a knock on the bathroom door and Nate's deep voice said, "Frankie...you okay in there?"

She had to swallow a couple of times before she managed a hoarse "I'm fine...go away," thankful that she would be able to blame the smoke for her red eyes and tight throat.

But the interruption had reminded her that crying never solved anything and she reached for the shampoo, determined to at least not look like a survivor of the Great Fire of London.

It took three washes to get the stench out of her hair and by the time she finally felt clean she noticed blood washing down the drain along with shampoo suds and shower cream.

She looked down at her feet and realized that the dressings had come loose. Oh, yeah, and she'd popped a few blisters on her right palm. Before she could start crying again, she reminded herself that it was okay, that these were things she could fix. Dressing a couple of cuts was basic stuff.

Everything else in her life? Well, that was another matter altogether.

She turned off the water and opened the shower door, reaching out to grab one of the thick fluffy towels that usually hung on the rail. When her hand grabbed air, she recalled that she'd left a pile of damp towels on her bedroom floor when she'd fallen into bed last night.

Great.

Huffing out an aggravated breath, she shoved dripping hair off her face and grabbed a hand towel, drying her hair as best she could before reaching for the hair towel—which of course wasn't large enough to adequately cover *anything.*

By the time she was reasonably dry, more blood stained the bathroom floor. But other than her towels, the only thing she had that would staunch the flow was her emergency stash of sanitary towels.

Shrugging, she reached into the cupboard under the basin. If football and hockey players could use tampons for nosebleeds, then there was nothing stopping her from using sanitary towels as makeshift pressure bandages.

Suitably padded up, Frankie covered the bare essentials with the tiny towel and hobbled painfully to the door. She pulled it open and stumbled back with a shocked squeak when she caught sight of a huge figure standing outside the door.

"What...what the...?" she rasped furiously, slapping one hand against her chest to keep her heart from making a break for it and the other on the wall, before recalling that her tiny towel needed help against the force of gravity.

Her shock turned to a panicked squawk as the towel slid silently southward. She made a frantic grab for it and caught sight of a wide, white grin at her futile efforts. The only course left to her was—

She grabbed for the door as a fiery blush covered every inch of exposed skin—of which there was a whole heap. For several seconds Frankie huddled behind the door, breathing like a racehorse after a two-mile gallop and coughing from all the smoke she'd inhaled that afternoon.

Finally, she caught her breath and peered around the door, half expecting to see Nate standing there, enjoying her discomfort. All she saw was a tanned muscular arm attached to a large hand holding out a pair of summer jammies.

She stared at the skimpy tank top and minuscule boy shorts for a couple of beats like they might bite her because this was a winter jammies kind of moment. The kind where a girl needed the comfort—and full-body concealment—of baggy flannel.

Considering it was either the towel or... With a muttered oath she reached out and snatched the tank and teeny shorts. She slammed the door to the sound of deep chuckles—*the jerk*—and hastily wrestled her PJs on, cursing herself for the way her body responded to the sound of that deep masculine sound.

Oh, yeah. And the fact that the man she'd once loved with every fiber of her eighteen-year-old being had just seen her naked.

In response, her skin was tight and sensitive, her breasts heavy and achy and...and the hot and heavy sensations turning her belly into a seething mess of dread, anticipation and nerves ratcheted her irritation up a couple gazillion notches.

She yanked open the door with a fierce scowl, only to find the passageway...empty.

"Seriously?" she muttered, before hightailing it to her bedroom for a sweatshirt because no way was she going down there looking like some sad attempt at a sex kitten. She heard a sound behind her and turned in time to see Nate standing on the top step, staring at her butt.

Resisting the urge to squirm or cover her bottom with both hands—heck, she wasn't *that* lame—Frankie cleared her ravaged throat and rasped in as cool a tone as she could manage, "Ex-*cu*-se me?"

Nate's gaze finally rose—crinkled at the corners as though he'd enjoyed running his eyes over her bottom and bare legs—and arched his brow at her tone. His eyes were unreadable, but with the knowledge that a minute ago he'd seen her *au naturel*—full frontal—Frankie felt her neck heat.

His amusement was soon replaced with a concerned frown as he stared at her feet.

"Your dressings came off."

Frankie shrugged and opened her mouth to say that it had been bound to happen, only to be interrupted by his curious "Are those...are those sanitary pads?" as he came closer. For some reason her blush deepened and she quickly turned away to hobble into her bedroom.

"They were handy," she called over her shoulder, heading to her closet for a zip-up sweater, which she hastily pulled on. Feeling a little more armed against his disturbingly intense gaze, she turned to find him filling the doorway, his hands shoved into his pockets.

Her heart leapt and then lodged in her throat because he looked like he was getting comfortable. And that meant—that meant her attempts to get rid of him had failed.

A shiver of something that couldn't possibly be pleasure, excitement and relief warred with irritation at his arrogance.

She scowled to cover her reaction. "What?"

"Lucky for you I'm handy too."

Her brow wrinkled. "If that is some sad attempt at seduction then you can just—"

He actually had the gall to laugh. "Relax, princess. I've had some training in field trauma so I'm sure I can handle a couple of bandages and burn gel."

"Don't be ridiculous. I'm an EMT. I can do it myself."

"Lucky for you, you don't have to," he countered mildly, stepping into the room. When she stubbornly glared at him, he murmured, "Either you go willingly or I sling you over my shoulder." His brow rose in challenge. "Your choice."

For a couple of beats Frankie considered defying him but the look in his eyes told her he wasn't kidding around. She uttered a growl of frustration and stomped toward him, hiding a wince at the pain in her feet.

"When did you get to be such a jerk?"

The question seemed to surprise him but he gave a soft snort before saying in a challenging voice, "When did I stop being a dupe, you mean?" His tone was wry. "You don't survive basic underwater demolition SEAL training by being a pushover, princess. Besides, what kind of friend would I be if I left you to fend for yourself?"

"The kind of friend who knows when I want to be alone," she said, trying not to show how much he was affecting her.

Nate made an exasperated sound in the back of

his throat and before she could respond in kind, he'd lifted her off her feet and swung her into his arms.

She gave a growl of protest and tried to wriggle free but his curt "Be still before you break both our necks," had her stiffening in his arms.

He carried her down the stairs as if she weighed no more than a child, muscles bunching beneath his warm, taut skin.

To cover the shiver that started at the base of her spine and shimmied up to the back of her neck…then spread everywhere else, she growled, "Drop me and you're dead meat."

His answer was an exasperated snort. "Please. I've carried twice your weight up a mountain pass that was more of a goat trail in a snowstorm." He briefly dropped his gaze. "But keep squirming like that and there's no telling what might happen."

Conscious of the arm beneath her butt and the press of her breasts against his hard chest, Frankie stopped squirming and tried to hang onto her bad mood.

"I see your arrogance hasn't improved," she

muttered, chagrined when amusement flashed in his gaze.

"No more than your reckless streak," he replied casually, but instead of getting annoyed she had to wonder if that was how people still saw her. And while it was true that she no longer did crazy things, she had to wonder if Nate truly believed Jack's death hadn't changed her.

Before she could ask, he placed her down on the kitchen counter and shoved a mug into her hands. "Drink," he ordered, turning away to look through her refrigerator. He made a sound of disgust and sent her a resigned look as he pulled his cellphone from his pocket. "When last did you go shopping?"

She thought about that a moment but couldn't remember.

He sighed. "Okay. Next question. When last did you eat?"

"Um…lemme see… This morning? Yep, this morning. I got breakfast delivered from Sid's. The delivery boy was rude and annoying."

"You probably forgot to tip him," he said.

"You can have the chocolate brownie," Frankie

said magnanimously. "As much as I love Sid's brownies, they're bad for my thighs."

She wanted to kick herself for mentioning her thighs when his gaze took a leisurely journey over them, his mouth kicking up at one corner as though recalling what she'd looked like standing in the bathroom doorway with her towel sliding to the floor. Or maybe when he'd checked out her legs in her pj shorts.

Hiding her embarrassment behind the mug in her hands, Frankie took a sip and grimaced at the taste. "What the heck is this? Are you trying to poison me?"

"SEAL remedy for whatever ails you. Drink up. By tomorrow you'll be as good as new." His look said she'd better do as he said. He turned away to concentrate on ordering takeout and Frankie waited until he disconnected to ask curiously, "Do you miss it? Being a SEAL, I mean."

His eyes instantly became hooded and just when she thought he didn't intend to answer, he said neutrally, "Not as much as I thought."

"What do you mean?"

His expression told Frankie he did miss it. She knew because Jack had once told her that military brotherhood was something that couldn't be explained. She knew it had something to do with having to trust and rely on each other in dangerous situations and that it made for very close ties.

His jaw bunched and his eyes turned flat. "I got tired of losing friends."

Recognizing his pain, she casually changed the subject, "So, do SEALs have magic secret remedies for everything?" wanting to breach the wall he'd abruptly erected between them.

He wrapped his warm hand around her left ankle and lifted her foot, studying her makeshift bandages. "We don't have one for stupidity." She went to jerk her foot away because it was clear he was done sharing, but Nate tightened his grip and removed the "bandage."

"Whoa," he said, when he saw the condition of her foot. "Don't you have any sense?"

"Apparently not," she muttered, finally noticing the medical supplies he'd set out on the kitchen table. "Or I'd have done a better job running you off my property."

"Not with these feet." He chuckled, shaking his head when she stuck her tongue out at him.

He hooked a chair with his boot and pulled it

closer, sitting so he could better see the bottom of her foot. She was tempted to plant her foot in his face and shove but he began to apply antiseptic cream and adhesive bandages with such gentleness that she was momentarily distracted.

"So…" she said casually, ignoring the tingles his long-fingered touch sent arrowing up her legs. "What's in this toxic beverage, anyway?"

His look was brief and amused. "If I told you I'd have to kill you."

Wrinkling her nose at him, she again considered kicking him but he was big and tough and her feet had been through enough. "You're a regular riot," she slurred, wondering why her tongue felt a little thick. The room spun lazily and she stared suspiciously at the mug. "Wha' ha' 'oo done?"

He rose fluidly and removed the mug from her nerveless fingers, catching her as she listed drunkenly. "Just a little herbal remedy, Red," he murmured, planting his wide shoulder against her midsection and lifting her as he rose to his full height. "Believe me, tomorrow you'll feel great."

Dizziness assailed her and she clutched at his back, fisting strangely lethargic hands in his shirt as he left the kitchen, walked down the passage and into the sitting room. He placed her carefully onto the couch, slid a couple of pillows beneath her head and pulled a blanket over her.

Frankie was already sliding into the comforting blackness when she remembered something she needed to say. "Nate?"

The air shifted and she cracked her eyes open to see that he'd dropped to his haunches beside her. "What is it, princess?"

For a long moment she stared into his familiar face and wondered at the strange emotions roiling inside her. He lifted a hand and carefully brushed her damp hair off her face, the gesture tender and full of familiarity and affection.

Despite the tears pricking the backs of her eyes, she felt her mouth curve and allowed her weighted eyelids to fall. "I'm glad you're home," she slurred sleepily. "I missed you, even if you did just slip me a mickey."

"You sure?" he teased softly. "Because it seems like you think I'm a pain in the butt."

"I don't mean it, Nate," she murmured, so softly he had to bend down to hear her. "It's just..." She gave a huge sigh that told him she was slipping into slumber. "'S just that you're a sexy BAB… and those're the ones a girl's gotta watch…or she's toast."

He grinned. "Don't you mean babe? As in sexy babe?"

"BAB," she slurred softly. "Badass boy. And you're pretty bad…ass."

Nate couldn't prevent a soft chuckle from escaping. "You're no slouch yourself, Red," he murmured, staring down into Frankie's face feeling a confusing mix of annoyance and affection that squeezed his chest and lodged right beside his heart.

He'd never met a more aggravating female—no, make that person—but Frankie had always had a soul-deep reservoir of sweetness that emerged at the oddest times.

And in a blinding moment of clarity he realized that, no matter what he'd done over the past fifteen years, or where he'd gone, she'd stayed with him. Their…connection had stayed with him.

And it scared him, because the people he was most attached to…had a habit of dying on him.

CHAPTER SEVEN

BY THE END of the week Frankie was tired of staying home, and because she was ready to climb the walls with frustration, she'd snapped at everyone who'd dropped in to visit. Everyone except Nate, that is. And that was only because he'd been conspicuously absent.

Bored out of her mind, she did a couple of loads of washing, vacuumed the downstairs, and discovered her phone—which she'd thought she'd lost the night of the storm—in a container of basmati rice in her pantry.

With a confused frown, she reached for it and decided she must have been really spaced out on meds to put it there.

It wasn't until she'd charged the battery and accessed her messages—all one hundred and forty-three of them—that seeds of suspicion began to grow. Then she read Terri's message:

Frankie, you gotta see this. It's awesome. Thanks for saving the big oaf. I owe you.

The instant she clicked on the link, she knew with certainty that *someone* had deliberately hidden her phone to keep her from seeing it. And she had a sneaking suspicion it was the one person who'd been conspicuously absent since the night he'd seen her naked and then drugged her with some funky-tasting SEAL potion.

Nate. The man featured in the video titled "Daring leap saves coastguard commander from certain death."

The instant the grainy images began playing, Frankie's eyes widened and her mouth dropped open. Chills snaked up her spine as she watched herself leap for Nate the instant he'd gone over and she felt sick once more at the thought of what could have happened.

They'd have been retrieving his body from the bottom of the gorge. And she'd have been dealing with yet another devastating loss.

Nate was bossy and annoying but she didn't want to contemplate a world without him in it.

She was still stewing when Paige arrived, laden down with bags from a local supermarket. She

let the other woman in and ignored her concerned frown as Paige headed for the kitchen
and dropped the bags on the table.

"Why is your face red like you're up to something illegal?" she demanded, placing her palm
on Frankie's forehead and checking her eyes.
"Are you sick? Have you been taking your antibiotics? I hear you haven't been to have your
wounds checked."

Frankie rolled her eyes. "I'm fine," she said
mildly, and folded her arms, propping her hip
against the counter. "Your turn to babysit?"

Paige made a half-hearted scoffing sound.
"Even if that were true—and it's not, because
you're a grown woman—you need your battle
wounds checked and I thought we could spend
some girl time together."

"So you're not here to cook for me just to make
sure I eat?"

Paige looked surprised for a moment before
resuming her chore with a snort. "Right." She
chuckled. "Like I cook. But don't worry, the doctor has just the thing for what ails you."

"Wine?"

"And other stuff." Paige beamed with delight. "We're going to have ourselves a party."

"What are we celebrating?"

The look Paige sent her was filled with censure. "Since when do we need a reason to drink wine, eat ice cream and watch chick flicks?"

Hours later, Frankie watched hockey on the sports channel while Paige slept, curled up on the sofa like she'd entered hibernation. They'd watched a rom com first, during which Frankie had sneered at the soppy moments, predicting exactly what would happen next and hooting with laughter at the clichéd dialogue.

At first Paige had tried to shush her but the plot had been so corny they'd ended up rewriting it in the most outrageous ways they could think of.

They'd made dinner and returned to watch an action adventure movie but Paige had soon fallen asleep. It was a movie Frankie had already seen so she'd switched over to sports.

The game had just gone into overtime when she heard a faint noise outside, followed by the clatter of a trash can falling over.

Grabbing her brother's old baseball bat, Frankie

padded to the front door and pressed her ear against the wood. Just when she thought the noise might have been one of the neighborhood raccoons, scavenging for an easy meal, she heard another thud, followed by soft cursing.

Whipping open the door, she stepped out and hefted the bat over her shoulder in a classic batter's stance. "Make another move, buster," she snarled, "and I'll use your head for batting practice."

Another curse had her tightening her grip and peering into the darkness as a large shadow materialized out of the night. Her pulse skipped a couple of beats and she swallowed a stupid girly squeak that would have mortified her if it had escaped.

Realizing that her neighborhood prowler was someone she knew, someone even more dangerous to her body and mind, Frankie demanded, "What are you doing sneaking around like a pervert?"

Nate lifted an arm to swipe at his face and it took only an instant to discover why. He was soaked, his uniform sticking to his skin like he was a hunky seal-a-meal.

Yum.

No, Frankie lectured herself silently, studying the man standing with one foot on the bottom step looking hotter than any man had a right to look in the middle of the night. *Not yum, dummy.* She was mad at him. Mad that kissing her and then seeing her naked had made him run away like she had a contagious disease.

"Run into any sprinklers while you were out playing covert ops in my garden?"

Nate made a rough sound of frustration in his throat and stomped up the stairs, his expression morphing from disgruntled to enquiring as he took in the baseball bat resting on her shoulder, her opposite hand resting on a canted hip.

"Expecting someone?"

"It's how I greet unwelcome guests," she replied smartly, sucking in a sharp breath when he came closer and the ambient light from inside illuminated his face. "What the heck, Nate?" she demanded, nudging him in his wide chest with the bat. "Have you been beating up the big boys at the Seafarers again?"

"Hey, careful with that," he complained, smoothly grabbing the bat as though he expected her to use it. Not that she wasn't tempted, but it looked like he'd just gone a couple of rounds with an LA street gang. "That was seventeen years ago and in case you haven't noticed, I *am* one of the big boys."

Of course she'd noticed. She'd have been an idiot not to see that he'd become a big badass boy. A name she'd called him—maybe—the other night in her drugged and weakened state.

She ran her gaze over him, telling herself that she wasn't noticing how his soaked clothes clung to every inch of muscle, sinew and bone, every inch of awesome masculine perfection.

"All I'm seeing is an idiot dripping on my ma—" She stopped abruptly when she noticed a darker stain marring the wet fabric of his shirt. "Omigod, you're...*bleeding*?"

He sighed and worked his jaw as though he was gritting his teeth. "It's nothing."

Nothing? Who was he kidding?

She sucked in a furious breath before saying tersely, "I'll be the judge of that," determined not to give him the satisfaction of falling apart like the silly heroine in the rom com she and Paige had watched earlier. But the awful truth was the sight of his blood instantly reminded her of how dangerous his job could be. Of how fragile human life really was. Of all the years worrying about him and Jack, only to have her worst fears confirmed with her brother's death.

"Come in and take off your boots," she ordered to cover her reaction. "I just cleaned."

He winced and held his side as he bent to unlace one tactical boot. "I thought you were supposed to be taking it easy."

"I was taking it easy," she retorted, bending to brush his hands aside so she could unfasten his boots herself. "I only vacuumed."

She watched as he toed the boots off and left them beside the door before he stepped inside.

"Paige here?" he asked.

"Why?" she demanded suspiciously, wondering if he'd come specifically so the doctor could fix him up. But, then, of course he had, she reminded herself irritably. And since he'd stayed away lately, she had to wonder if he'd been worried she'd get romantic ideas.

"Her car's in the driveway. I was about to leave when I heard the trash can go over and decided to check it out." He entered the kitchen and squinted in the bright light. "Since when do you open a door without first checking who it is?"

"Shh," Frankie warned in a low tone. "Paige is sleeping. I was about to head off to bed when I heard you stumbling around like the three stooges after an all-night bender."

"I'm too old for benders and I'll have you know I'm an expert at moving among the enemy without them ever knowing I've been there."

She didn't want to think about him sneaking around enemy territory. It gave her nightmares and made her act badly.

"You've clearly lost your edge," she snorted, ruthlessly suppressing a quiver when his eyes went dark. Dark in a look she knew all too well. Maybe hadn't *seen* in a good long while, but still recognized—especially when his mouth curved into a sensual smile that had her knees wobbling and her belly doing the Highland fling on hot coals.

For years she'd watched him ensnare women of all ages with his dark good looks and bad-boy smile, but he'd never looked at *her* as anything but Jack Bryce's little sister.

She swallowed. How the heck was she supposed to handle this older, hotter, brooding version of the boy she'd once adored? A man with sexy eyes and sexier mouth?

"Ya think?" he drawled dryly, but there was an edge to his voice that confused Frankie and she turned away before he saw exactly how he affected her. Limping to the refrigerator, she yanked it open, wondering if this was his way of keeping her off balance.

That it was working annoyed her no end.

"What are you doing here at this time of night looking like…?" She waved her hand at his face. "Like that?"

Nate had done a lot of crazy stuff in his lifetime, often—tonight, for instance—disregarding his own safety to protect others. But he'd never made a habit of visiting women where he wasn't sure of his welcome.

He'd been with a lot of sophisticated, beautiful woman but when he'd looked up and seen Frankie standing on her porch, the light spilling over her body like she was a kickass heroine in an action movie, it had hit him right between the eyes.

Standing there with her legs spread for balance,

a baseball bat gripped in one hand and resting on her shoulder, she'd made his world tilt on its axis. Her hair was wild and messy and as far as he could see there wasn't a lick of makeup on her face. Her natural beauty was patently obvious.

It reminded him of exactly why he'd stayed away—because he wasn't nearly as immune to her as he'd thought. But, then, he hadn't meant to come here at all, fully intending to go home to a hot shower and bed.

Weary, he leaned against the counter and watched as she reached into the refrigerator to pull out a beer. He didn't even want to think about the fact he was suddenly allowing himself to see her as the sexiest woman he'd ever met. She was annoying, reckless, contrary and could be downright belligerent when she wanted to be.

But she was also tall and curvy, every man's living fantasy, even dressed in snug shorts, a baggy T-shirt and thick socks. She'd also piled her luxurious red-gold curls atop her head in a style that was both messy and incredibly appealing.

His hands itched to explore but before he could reach out and bury his fingers in the heavy mass, she turned and silently handed him the beer. With a look that was hard to read, she disappeared down the passage, leaving him to wonder if she'd seen where his gaze had been.

Not that he cared, Nate assured himself. He was a red-blooded male over thirty and could look where he wanted.

Except there, a voice in his head reminded him. *There you'll find only trouble.*

But Nate ignored the voice and tried to decide what it was about her that kept throwing him off balance. She was all grown up, sure, and there was still that streak of recklessness…but she'd changed.

Or maybe…maybe his years in the SEALs—seeing and doing things ordinary people couldn't imagine—had changed *him*. And perhaps *that* had changed the way he saw her. Maybe he was being kept off balance by the brief flashes he saw of that lively young girl in the very put-together woman she'd become.

Before he could ponder it further, she was back with her emergency medical kit, demanding "What?" when she caught his somber gaze.

He shook his head and the sensation of his

world tilting on its axis faded. "I wanted to tell you before you heard it from someone else." He paused, wondering how to mention the other big headache in his life. The video that made *her* look like a kickass superhero and him…well, not so much.

She put the backpack on the table and flashed him a wary look. Free of cosmetics, her skin was smooth and dewy and infinitely touchable.

"Tell me what?"

He lifted a hand to scratch his jaw, wondering why he was noticing her skin now. Deep down he knew, though. After that kiss…the taste, scent and feel of her skin had been burned into his mind and his senses.

Realizing what he was thinking, Nate lifted a hand to massage the band of tension tightening around his skull.

Get a grip.

"There's a video clip online," he growled, wondering what he'd thought he was doing when he'd found himself outside her house. He should have put his truck back in gear and got out of there. He should have listened to his gut, which had been screaming like a five-alarm fire. But, no. He'd had to go all super-soldier when he'd heard the trash can falling. As though he *wanted* to be the hero Frankie said she didn't want or need.

She gave a short derisive laugh and for a horrifying moment he thought he'd voiced his thoughts out loud.

"What?"

Her gaze was mocking. "I've seen it, Nathan. Terri beat you to it."

"How did you— Never mind." He sighed and rubbed the back of his neck where his muscles bunched with tension and fatigue. "Just don't answer any calls or talk to anyone. Publicity will handle it."

She unzipped the emergency kit and began pulling out supplies. "I know you hid my phone," she said, flashing him a look that dared him to deny it. "And swore everyone to silence." She narrowed her gaze. "The question is why?"

Nate watched her toss a packet of alcohol swabs onto the table. He didn't want to analyze his actions so he went with, "I didn't hide it. I put it in rice because it was wet and forgot to tell you." It was the truth. Just not the full truth, which was that he'd looked like a rookie who had needed saving.

Her snort conveyed her opinion of his lame explanation. "Are you sure it wasn't because the big badass SEAL needed saving...by a girl?"

"Of course not." He managed a chuckle, thinking that Frankie had always been too sharp and perceptive for her own good. "I think my ego and rep can handle that." He broke off to yawn. "Besides, you needed the rest."

"Looks like you should take your own advice."

His mouth twisted into a wry smile. "Yeah, well." He rubbed a hand over his face before murmuring, "Hard to get any rest when you're boarding dark unmarked vessels carrying human cargo."

Frankie stilled and her eyes widened. "You mean like...traffickers? Here? In Port St. John's?"

Nate grunted and folded his arms across his chest, wincing at the pain radiating from where a bullet had grazed him. He'd been conducting night stealth training when they'd come across the battered vessel a little too close to the coast for comfort.

"We intended to surprise the crew, only to find

illegals hoping to sneak into Canada via the islands."

"Does MSRT handle that sort of thing?"

"If there's a threat alert but we were already out on maneuvers and decided to check it out." He ran his fingers through his hair, scattering water droplets in every direction.

Eyes searching, she gestured to his face. "Is that where you got on the wrong end of a fist, Commander I-Used-to-be-a-Badass-Navy-SEAL?"

His mouth twitched because a teasing Frankie was always hard to resist. "It's Lieutenant Commander, as you well know. And I'm still a badass."

She smirked but ignored the chastisement, asking instead, "Hungry?"

"You offering to cook me a meal, Red?"

She rolled her eyes and made a scoffing sound. "In your dreams. I only cook for people I like."

He allowed a smile to tease the corner of his mouth and addressed the issue—or *one* of the issues—between them. "Is that why you told me the other night that you were glad I was home? Because you don't like me? Or is it because I'm a sexy BAB?"

Wild color appeared beneath her creamy skin, making him want to touch it, see if it was as soft and warm as it looked. "Don't be ridiculous," she drawled ironically. "I was drugged out of my mind. Besides, I thought you were someone else."

Nate just chuckled because he knew she was lying; knew she was embarrassed by the momentary vulnerability.

"There's leftovers from dinner," she continued after a hard stare. "Why don't you ditch the wet clothes while I rummage around?"

"Did...did I hear you right?" he demanded, pretending to be shocked. "Did you just tell me to undress?" He waited until she lifted her gaze. "Trying to get me naked by offering to feed me, Francis?"

She rolled her eyes. "You forget I've seen you in swimwear, Nate," she drawled smoothly, and turned away, but he caught the deepening flush that rose up the back of her neck. "Nothing I haven't seen before."

He gave a soft snort and reached for his buttons, reminding himself that the reason he was removing his shirt was because he'd been wearing a wetsuit instead of tactical gear when he'd climbed aboard the unmarked vessel.

Immediately sensing something off, he'd reacted a split second before gunfire had erupted from the stern. He'd shoved the rookie with him aside but hadn't managed to avoid the bullet himself. Fortunately, it had just grazed him but his fall over the trash can outside had reopened the wound and it had begun bleeding again.

"That was over a decade ago," he said referring to her insult about his body. "Before I joined the SEALs."

"Don't be ridiculous. I saw you—" She went abruptly quiet, as though realizing what she'd been about to admit. "On second thoughts, you're right." She waved her hand, dipping her head to pretend interest in the medical supplies, which meant some red-gold curls slid across her rosy cheek to hide her expression.

Amused by her reaction, he said softly, "Been spying on me, Red?"

She stiffened, high color staining the edge of her cheekbones. He doubted many people got to see Francis Abigail Bryce blush. "Th-that's... that's ridiculous," she spluttered in outrage. "It's not spying if you're strutting around half-naked in public for everyone to see."

"Public?" His eyes narrowed in confusion that quickly cleared when he remembered catching her and Paige—along with half the female population of PSJ—hanging over the boardwalk railing, watching beach training and cheering them on a few weeks ago. "Oh, right." He chuckled. "Beach training."

"And it wasn't you I was looking at, anyway. So don't go getting a big head." She swept a scornful gaze over his wet T, her expression changing to one of horror when she caught sight of the blood staining his shirt. "And, dammit, Nate, I thought you were done being a hero."

"It's my job, Francis. I was a little off my game, that's all. Besides," he continued impatiently, because the reason he'd been off his game was standing there looking sexy and annoyed. He never used to have problems focusing, but lately he'd been preoccupied. It scared him because if being in the teams had taught him one thing, it was that when a man allowed himself to be distracted people died.

He'd nearly died a week ago because he'd

dropped onto that ledge and found not just any rescue worker but the woman he'd promised to protect. But how the heck was he expected to look out for her if she was still wild and reckless?

"It's just a scratch."

After a brief battle of stares, Frankie snapped, "Fine. Then you won't mind if I check it myself."

He silently weighed his options and decided that letting her patch him up was better than a trip to ER.

He sighed and shed his outer shirt. Reaching for the T, he sucked in a sharp breath when he felt Frankie's smooth, warm fingers brush his wet skin.

For a blinding moment he imagined she was undressing him for something entirely different but then his head cleared because her expression was anything but seductive as she grabbed the hem and lifted. He was forced to raise his arms or get whacked on the nose and took over with a warning growl, whipping the shirt over his head while Frankie muttered something about a "shoddy patch-up job."

Annoyed because he'd done it himself, he demanded, "You think you can do better?"

"Of course I can do better," she snapped, sounding offended. "I have several advanced diplomas to say that I can do better." She carefully pulled away the clumsy bandage and sucked in a sharp breath.

"Omigod!" Her gaze rose to his, stunned and furious. *"That* is no scratch."

CHAPTER EIGHT

NATE SIGHED AND waited in resignation for her
to state the obvious. He didn't have to wait for
more than a couple of beats.

"You've been *shot*?" Frankie accused, her voice
rising. "You've been shot and you didn't tell me?"

"It's no big deal—" he began, only to become
distracted by the luxurious length of her lashes
and the way they made thick lacy curtains on
her cheeks. He was so entranced by them it was
a couple of seconds before he noticed that her
moss green eyes had turned stormy.

Stormy and sexy and—

"You let me think it was a matter of you being
clumsy," she clipped out tersely, totally dispel-
ling the idiotic vision growing inside his head.
A vision that was far more dangerous than getting shot by modern-day pirates.

Nate blinked to dispel the sensual web she was

weaving around him and sucked in air to clear his head because *what the hell was he thinking*?

"It's no big deal," he growled, lifting a hand to pinch the bridge of his nose. He was more annoyed at himself than at her and was starting to wish he'd never given in to the stupid impulse to come.

Before he could explain, a sleepy Paige appeared in the doorway. "What's going on? I heard voices… Oh," she said, spying him. "Hi, Nate."

Grateful for the interruption, Nate turned his attention to the petite doctor. "Hey, Dr. P. How's it going?"

She took in the sight of him sitting shirtless on the table, and Frankie standing with an alcohol swab in her hand looking like she was contemplating murder.

"Better than you apparently." Her brow wrinkled as she wandered closer, going still when she saw his injury up close. "That's a—" Her eyes widened as what she was seeing dawned on her. Her mouth dropped open and the sleepy look vanished. "You…you've been shot? What happened? Why didn't you go to the ER?"

"See," Frankie said curtly, jabbing a finger at

him. "I'm not the only one who knows a gunshot wound when they see one."

He grabbed her hand before she could drill him with a fingernail.

"I didn't go to the ER because it's no big deal," he growled, wondering at the jumble of confusing emotions making him behave like an idiot who didn't know the score. Especially the ones that urged him to pull Frankie close and prove just how okay he was. And maybe have those long-fingered hands slide all over his body.

Stunned by the abrupt need knifing through him, Nate dropped her hand and scrubbed a hand over his face, hoping to scrub away the images in his mind. Maybe he was just tired, because there was no way he was contemplating tangling with Frankie.

No way.

"I've had worse. A lot worse."

His assurances did nothing to appease her. She looked ready to punch him. "Seriously, Nate," she snapped, her eyes going all squinty, "now is *not* the time to remind me how much you like playing hero."

He opened his mouth to deny he'd been a hero

but she ignored him, muttering something about heroes being no good to anyone when they're dead, and he knew she was referring to Jack.

"This was just me being clumsy, really," he soothed when she looked ready to snatch his beer bottle away. "I didn't get out of the way in time."

She spun away, eyes shadowed and her mouth pressed in a tight line of unhappiness. "What about next time, genius?"

He sighed and reached out to brush escaped strands of silky curls off her face but she jerked away, looking like she might bite his hand off at the wrist. He suppressed a smile mostly because, despite her insistence that she didn't like heroes, she'd been drawn to saving people too.

Tipping the bottle to his mouth, he taunted softly, "Aw. Worried you'll miss me, Francis?"

She reacted just as he'd predicted. "Don't be an idiot," she snapped, and he suppressed a private little smile that at least some things hadn't changed. But then she sprayed his side with disinfectant and demanded, "Why would I miss you? You're annoying and juvenile and—"

"There won't be a next time," he interrupted, hissing out a pained breath when he realized she'd used Merthiolate to cleanse his side. Probably because—*yowza*—it would sting more than a million fire ants.

With her eyes hot and upset, she demanded, "How can you know that, Nate?"

"Next time I'll be in full tactical gear," he rasped through gritted teeth. "Any stray bullets will do nothing but make a hole in my vest. And maybe if you're lucky, a nice bruise to remind me what an idiot I am."

"If they have any brains they'd aim for your stupid head," she muttered, squeezing a generous amount of antibiotic cream along the shallow furrow and confirming his suspicions that she'd used Merthiolate to punish him.

He caught her hand to get her attention. "Did you hear the words *tactical gear*, Francis?"

"No," she snapped, pulling away and taking the large adhesive bandage Paige handed her. "All I heard was blah, blah, blah… I'm a stupid macho idiot, trying to get myself killed."

"Jack didn't *deliberately* get himself killed, Frankie," he said gently. "It's just a hazard of the job. A hazard we all accept."

"Not me," she rasped. "And you shouldn't either."

Battling frustration, Nate dropped her hand and shoved his fingers through his hair, resisting the urge to pull out chunks because dealing with Francis always made him a little crazy.

"Well, there's a tactical helmet too," he continued as though she hadn't spoken. "It won't stop a point-five slug, but pretty much everything else."

Paige was silent throughout the exchange and when Frankie fell into a fuming silence she asked Nate, "You okay?"

"Never better," he practically snarled.

Amusement tugged at the corners of her sleepy mouth and her hazel eyes sparkled with amusement. "I can see that." She shifted her attention back to Frankie. "Need any help?"

"I've got this," Frankie said curtly. "You go back to sleep. You're off the clock and there's no need to patch up idiots in your free time."

"You're sure you don't need me…?" She paused a moment and when Frankie shook her head, she nodded and said, "Okay, then," and cleared her throat as though fighting a laugh. She looked around. "Have you seen my car keys?"

Frankie's head came up. "You're leaving?"

"Hmm?" Paige said, looking around absently.

"Exhausting day in the ER on top of the baby clinic." She gave a huge yawn that looked suspiciously fake. "I could sleep for a week. Besides, you're a disgustingly early riser and I want to sleep in tomorrow morning."

Before Nate could ask the petite doctor what she was up to, Frankie said, "You don't have to go. Nate is leaving."

"No, I'm not," he contradicted mildly. "You said you'd feed me. Plus, I figured that you owe me for getting injured chasing down bad guys for you."

"It's okay," Paige said on a chuckle, and leaned forward to kiss Nate on the cheek. "Don't go catching any more bullets, big guy, you're clearly not bulletproof." She hugged Frankie, said "I'll see myself out," and disappeared down the passage. There was a short silence before they heard the sound of the front door closing.

Frankie frowned and looked at the wall clock.

He wondered why he hadn't taken the opportunity to escape when it had presented itself. Clearly he wasn't as smart as all his advanced engineering degrees said he was. He silently drank his beer while Frankie applied a couple of Steri-Strips to the cuts on his face.

Sound filtered through from the TV that was still on in the sitting room but otherwise the house was quiet.

And then it hit him.

They were alone…in a dark, empty house in the middle of the night.

Not only were they alone but, despite Frankie's attitude, he had a feeling that she was just as determined to ignore the simmering tension, just waiting for one wrong move from either of them to explode.

"Relax," he said wearily, wondering if he was referring to Paige having headed out on her own or…well, the growing tension between them. "This is Port St. John's. People don't get blown up here, Francis."

"But—"

"Believe me, I've seen bad and this isn't it."

She frowned, clearly not convinced.

Nate studied her beautiful face; close enough that if he wanted to he could turn his head and their lips would touch.

He froze, the beer bottle halfway to his mouth.

Where had these dangerous thoughts come from all of a sudden? Because they were the absolute last thing he needed right now, especially as he had enough problems juggling all the other responsibilities in his life. Messing with Frankie would be both stupid *and* dangerous.

She frowned. "You okay?"

Oh, yeah he was great, just great. He'd left the SEALs because he'd lost too many people he cared about. He'd transferred to the US Coast Guard for the same reason—to protect those he loved. His mom, Terri, Ty and Paige, and all their friends and colleagues…and Frankie. He couldn't do that if he allowed himself to get distracted. Which meant… His jaw clenched. It meant that he needed to stay away.

For her sake as well as his.

"Peachy."

Which also meant that he had to leave now. Because resisting Frankie's grown-up allure was becoming increasingly difficult. Especially as they were alone in a darkened house and he hadn't participated in any recreational activities with a woman in far too long.

Staying was just asking for the kind of trouble he didn't need or want.

Coming to an abrupt decision, Nate placed the half-empty beer bottle on the table and with a palm flat against her belly he nudged her back a couple of paces, slid off the table and reached for his wet shirts.

He caught her baffled frown out of the corner of his eye. "Where are you going? I haven't finished. Besides, I thought you were hungry."

He studied her face silently before turning to head for the front door as fast as he could. "Oh, I am, princess," he tossed over his shoulder. "But not for food."

After a short stunned silence, she demanded behind him, "What's that supposed to mean?"

With frustration beating at him, he drawled roughly, "It means that if I stay I'll take you up on more than your offer of free medical care and leftovers."

He heard her sharply indrawn breath and turned in time to catch the odd look that flashed across her face before a shutter came down, hiding her thoughts from him. Instead, amused challenge replaced the soft, uncertain—very un-Frankie-like—expression.

"Oh, please," she scoffed, folding her arms beneath her breasts and cocking one hip to the side. "The big badass Navy SEAL can't *handle* anything more than leftovers. Not that I'm offering," she said pointedly. "Especially not to you. Not again. Not ever."

Ignoring her reference to her eighteenth birthday, he drawled mockingly, "I don't accept *anyone*'s leftovers, princess. I'm an all-or-nothing kind of guy."

But right now none of that mattered because her pose reminded him that barely five days ago he'd seen her naked. Naked and lush and every man's fantasy. Something that had tormented him because he knew he wouldn't get another chance.

Shouldn't get another chance if he intended to keep his promise to his friend. He needed to keep his mind on his job. People depended on him to keep them safe. Not just his mother and sister—but his men too.

Then she challenged his masculinity with a taunted "You couldn't handle it anyway, Nate." And something snapped inside his head.

Knowing he was making a mistake and suddenly not caring—because, God knew, she drove him completely insane—he retraced his steps, stalking her like a leopard stalked its unwary prey.

Something in his expression had her backing up a step and putting out her hand like a traffic cop. Dark amusement joined the frustration because she actually thought that would stop him.

She was right to be wary, because something dark and tumultuous was driving him.

"Are you sure about that, princess?" he drawled softly, advancing slowly, forcing her to retreat another step. "You're not the only one who's changed. How do you even know what I can handle anymore?"

When she realized he'd all but boxed her in between the wall and the coat rack, she growled, her eyes narrowing a warning that he ignored. To her credit she didn't try to escape, instead letting him advance until his chest bumped against her outstretched palm.

"Nate," she said, tilting her head to stare at him as though he'd grown three heads. "What are you doing?"

Yeah, Nate. What are *you doing?*

Ignoring her and the voice in his head, Nate stepped in, pushing her against the wall, forcing her hand to flatten against his chest. And as he stared into the darkening depths of her moss green eyes, the heat of her palm seeped into his flesh and spread warmth and warning across his skin.

He welcomed the warmth…ignored the warning.

"I'm showing how much you don't know about me, babe."

Her back snapped straight and she thrust out her chin.

"Oh, please," she scoffed. "You're a man. You couldn't handle me as a child. What makes you think you can handle me now, Commander Big Shot?"

Fire began to race across his skin. Against his better judgment he found that he loved that about her—that damn-your-eyes challenge. His muscles tightened and bunched and the skin across his scalp prickled. But Nate was accustomed to ignoring distractions and focusing on his mission. Mostly.

Right now his mission was to warn her off—*hell*, warn himself off.

"Someday, princess," he murmured, reaching up to brush his knuckles along the clean line of her jaw, "someone might take that challenge seriously."

She gasped in outrage, her eyes flashing with a defiance that lit a slow-burning fuse to his long-buried need.

"Oh, yeah?" she rasped, giving him a not-so-gentle shove. "And I suppose you think *you're* the man to do it?"

A rough laugh escaped him, his gaze drifting from her defiant green eyes to her soft mouth. "I'm not *that* crazy, princess. You think you're tough enough to take me on, but you aren't. Nowhere near."

Shoving him with both hands this time, she growled, "And *you* are, Commander I-Think-I'm-So-Tough?"

His heart rate doubled and his skin prickled a primitive warning that he ignored because he suddenly knew why he'd come tonight. He wanted—no, *needed*—this…this wild flood of reckless exhilaration. Something he hadn't experienced in too long.

"I'm plenty tough, Red." He leaned forward to growl in her ear. "Now…" his mouth brushed against her neck and he felt her go still, her breath hitching in her throat as though she couldn't believe his audacity. His mouth curved against her soft skin "…let's see just how tough *you* are."

The tension thickened and Nate swore he could see sparks zipping through the air between them. He opened his mouth on her delicate skin and a voice in the back of his mind yelled, *Pull back, pull back.*

But then Frankie's nails dug furrows in the skin of his chest and the warning abruptly faded. Drawing back, his gaze locked on her mouth a couple of inches beneath his, the curves soft, plump, moist…*inviting*. Then her breath quickened in the heated silence and with a muttered curse Nate caught her mouth in a punishing kiss. Although who he'd intended to punish wasn't so clear, especially when the taste of her filled his mouth and—*oh, yeah*—sent his senses reeling.

She gasped as though he'd caught her by surprise. *Hell*, he'd surprised himself too, so sure that he could taunt her and then leave, unscathed.

He still could, he assured himself. He'd kiss her breathless and rid himself of this overwhelming need crushing his resistance, making him forget long-held promises. And because he felt driven by something buried too deep to analyze, he wanted to teach her that messing with him came with consequences.

Consequences he suddenly couldn't recall, but was all too willing to face…later.

Much later.

Once he'd had his fill.

Thrusting his hands in her hair to hold her so he could wage a sensual war on her soft, pliable mouth, Nate promised himself that he would leave soon. After another few tastes…another few deep drugging kisses…then he would leave. Just as he had last time. Besides, he was the master of control, the master of his own destiny. And he'd prove it.

In another minute.

Frankie gave a shocked, furious gasp and managed to shove him back a couple of inches, her gaze fiery and defiant. But as their ragged breathing filled the quiet hallway, her warmth seeped into his skin, setting off a chain reaction that could have only one conclusion.

Frankie's entire system jolted as his kiss had her gasping in outrage and a wild excitement that had her pulse trebling and her senses scattering like autumn leaves.

Hot prickles flashed across her skin as Nate captured her hands and pinned them to the wall next to her head, and she had no idea what it said about her that she was a second away from orgasm.

"Get *off* me...you big...*oaf*," she snarled breathlessly, horrified that her limbs had turned to cooked noodles and that her belly was clenching with alarm and anticipation.

Anticipation?

No way. There was no way she was anticipating tangling with Nate, physically or verbally.

But deep down she knew—*oh, boy, did she know*—that she was lying. Every strand of DNA rejoiced that she was once again up close and personal with all that hard flesh and satin-warm skin.

CHAPTER NINE

WITH NATE PLASTERED to her and her hands trapped, there was only one thing left for Frankie to do.

Turning her head, she sank her teeth into his naked shoulder and bit down. Hard. If she'd expected him to curse and pull back, she was a little surprised when he just laughed, a deep thrilling sound that sent tingles scattering across her skin, liquefying her bones and laying siege to her resistance.

His hard thigh flexed between hers, blasting heat deep in her belly. Muscles clenching against the shockingly intense sensations, Frankie knew she needed to do something before he swept away all her resistance.

Drugged by the taste of him in her mouth, she bit him harder. Nate simply flexed his shoulder and taunted softly, "Like what you taste, Red?" in her ear. And even if his breathing was as ragged as hers, it was Frankie who shuddered because he was right. She did like what she tasted. In fact, she was hungry for more.

"Because, let me tell you," he breathed and gently closed his teeth on the skin between her neck and shoulder, searing a line of fire across her flesh that landed with a jolt in her liquid center, "I sure like the taste of *you*."

A shaft of panic sliced through the ratcheting excitement. *If he doesn't leave soon,* she thought, *there's no telling what I'll do.* Not with the equal mix of fury, pleasure and anticipation pouring through her.

"Y-you…y-you…" *Really? Now you're stammering?* Sucking in a ragged breath, Frankie steadied herself, determined not to let him know how he affected her. "I know you, Nate," she rasped defensively. "You're only doing this to punish me for daring to challenge your fragile male ego."

He stilled and for an instant she thought her words had done what her struggles could not— send him out the door. But then he lifted those sexy dark-gold eyes, glowing with a wild recklessness that was terrifyingly exhilarating.

Kind of like free-falling out an airplane at fifty thousand feet.

"Is that what you think, babe?" he murmured, dipping his head to swipe his tongue across her bottom lip. "Just goes to show that you don't know me at all."

A sob of need caught in her throat but the last thing she wanted or needed was to be vulnerable to him. Frankie didn't do vulnerable. For any man. Especially a man who'd already crushed her tender heart.

"I don't want you," she snarled, twisting her head to evade his tormenting mouth. *Why the heck did he have to be so darn...irresistible?*

"Little liar," he breathed on a soft chuckle. "You want me. You want me bad."

"Why you arrogant, self-important—" she spluttered, only to have her words cut off when he opened his mouth over hers in a kiss that just about knocked her socks right off her feet. It started out as a hard, demanding kiss that quickly escalated into a hot mating of mouths that sucked the breath out of her lungs.

With a low helpless moan, she strained closer. Nate tightened his grip on her and sucked her bottom lip into his mouth, knowing just how to render her a helpless, quivering blob of sensual need.

"Nate," she gasped, feeling her knees buckle, feeling the hot ache in her core build until it was all she could do to keep from moving against the hard thigh between hers, against the growing evidence of his arousal. "*Nate*…s-stop."

No, don't stop. Don't ever stop... Because he was big and thick and hard against her. And getting bigger and thicker and harder by the second and…and she hadn't felt this good in a long time.

"Stop?" he teased softly, clearly preoccupied with tasting her skin, helping himself to her mouth; because instead of stopping he hummed in the back of his throat and moved to another spot. "You sure that's what you want, babe?"

Of course she wasn't sure. Only that it would be smart because after Jack's death Frankie had promised to make smarter choices with her life. Choices that didn't include being vulnerable. To anyone.

Then Nate's thigh flexed, dragging a ragged whimper from her throat.

"See," he murmured softly, his mouth tormenting hers. "It's too late for that, Red. Way...too... late."

And then he released her wrists, sliding his big hands down her arms, her sides, to grasp and lift when he reached her bottom, forcing her to wrap her legs around him. Then he settled, big and hot and hard right where she ached, and she was about a second away from orgasm even though they hadn't even reached the good part yet.

Nate tightened his grip and took the kiss deeper...deeper, hotter and bolder than any she'd ever experienced. And before she knew it, Frankie was moving against him, making embarrassingly hungry sounds that might have mortified her if he hadn't growled a response that was as hungry as hers.

She'd forgotten what it was like to be kissed with such savage hunger. Okay, so maybe she'd *never* been kissed with such single-minded intensity—as though he wanted to consume her. Or maybe make her forget every other kiss she'd ever received.

It was working because she couldn't even recall her own name, let alone anything else. When he finally broke the kiss and pulled back, his breathing was as ragged as hers.

"Francis…" he breathed.

And she thought, *Oh, yeah, that's it. That's my name.* But then she became aware of his heart, pounding against hers with the same jagged rhythm.

"No talking," she ordered, fisting his hair and pulling his mouth back to hers.

His lips curved. "Francis…"

"I said no talking," she growled irritably. Because if she let him talk, he might change his mind…and she might remember what a bad idea it was to let Nathan Oliver into her life again.

He chuckled at the same moment he rocked his hips into hers, drawing a low moan from her throat.

Nate gave a laugh and backed away from the wall. He took a few steps toward the stairs then stopped. One hand slid up her back to fist her messy topknot. He pulled her back a couple of inches and growled, "This *is* what you want?"

She blinked at the question. Was he kidding? Of course this was what she wanted. Couldn't he feel how much she wanted him? *She* could certainly feel how much he wanted *her*.

"Frankie."

She didn't know why her nickname on his lips did something to her but she stopped trying to get at his mouth. One look into his searching, solemn gaze had her hands sliding up to cup his strong jaw. "Yes," she said with a certainty that couldn't be misunderstood.

His unreadable gaze remained on hers for a long moment before going as hot as the sinfully badass smile curving his mouth. "All right, then," he murmured, and bounded up the stairs as though he wasn't carrying a woman taller than most men. It both shocked and excited her, eliciting a gasping laugh as she tightened her thighs, only to instantly loosen them again when she recalled that just a half hour ago she'd treated his bullet wound.

"Your side," she managed to croak.

Only to be interrupted by his grunted "Is fine," as he tightened his arms, pressing a most impressive erection against her. The jolt of electricity had her eyes crossing and her back arching.

She managed a stuttered, "B-but—" before

closing her teeth on his shoulder again when she realized to her horror that she sounded all breathless and desperate.

His growled response filled her darkened bedroom as he headed unerringly for her bed—as though he could see in the dark. Probably could, she thought, giving a startled yelp when she flew through the air to land in a graceless tangle of limbs and pillows in the middle of it.

She lay blinking up at him, a large, dangerous presence in the dark room. And although she knew he'd never hurt her, a quiver of unease moved through her. Partly because there was always the fear that he'd leave her in a state of raging hormonal discomfort—as he had the night he'd kissed her senseless on her doorstep then sauntered off to his stupid truck—but mostly because when it came to Nate Oliver, she'd always been vulnerable.

He moved, but instead of leaving he leaned forward. Soft light spilled across the bed and just like that all Frankie's girlish insecurities returned. She was once again that skinny, freckled girl wishing she was like the beach babes Nate gravitated toward and hating herself for wanting to be one of a crowd.

Maybe she wasn't that girl, hadn't been that girl for a good long while, but she still found herself looking down at the less-than-attractive picture she made in her ratty oversize T-shirt and thick socks. How pathetic was that?

She felt the skin across her forehead tighten. She hadn't meant for this to happen, and she was fairly certain neither had he, but maybe—

"Francis...condom?"

For one panicked moment she couldn't remember the last time she'd even needed one—*even more pathetic*—before another thought occurred—this one much more satisfying. "You don't carry condoms?" His gaze narrowed. "I thought SEALs always came prepared?"

He made a rough sound of impatience and shoved shaking—*yeah, they were shaking*—fingers through his hair, but even in the low light Frankie could detect the faint redness creep up his neck.

"Top drawer," she snickered, and watched as he yanked open the drawer with barely leashed violence. He didn't comment on the fact that the box was unopened and she snatched it from him to tear impatiently at the packaging.

It abruptly gave way, scattering condoms over the bed and across the floor.

Nate gave a low laugh as he snatched up a small foil square. "Impatient much, babe?" he rasped, and tossed it to her.

"Lose the pants, Oliver," she ordered, and when he didn't react fast enough, she reached out impatiently. The next few moments were a flurry of hands until Frankie became distracted by his eight pack, by the cut muscles on the sides of his hips and the way his skin felt beneath her fingers—all hot and taut and smooth.

She gently ran a fingernail around the startling white dressing over his wound, her mouth curving with delight as goose bumps broke out across his skin.

Nate cursed, a sound pain-filled and impatient. It had her hands stilling and her hungry gaze rising, past his defined abs and pecs, his shoulders, up his strong tanned throat and hard jaw to his dark, burning gaze.

It promised a universe of sensual punishment.

Frankie gulped. "Does it hurt?"

"Don't feel a thing." His mouth curved in a wicked smile. "Well, not there, anyway."

Rolling her eyes, she leaned forward and swiped her tongue across the taut skin south of his abs, delighting in his sharply indrawn breath and the fine tremor in the fingers that gripped her shoulders.

She gave in to the urge to nip his belly too, laughing at Nate's ragged curse. The next instant he shoved her back onto the bed and pushed his pants and boxer briefs to his feet. His erection sprang free, big and thick and hard, but Frankie had only a couple of seconds to admire it before he was joining her on the bed.

"You're overdressed," he growled, pushing her flat and sliding his big palms up her thighs to the curve of her bottom. She tried to sit up, get her mouth and hands on him, but Nate made a sound of impatience and pressed her flat.

Capturing her wrists, he lifted them over her head, ratcheting her excitement up a couple dozen notches.

"Dammit, Nate," she grunted breathlessly. "I want to—"

"Shh," he murmured, pinning her with one

heavily muscled leg and silencing her protests with his hot mouth.

The kiss—a lush, deep mating of mouths—made her forget her need to control things and she found herself kissing him back like a starving person.

Gradually the hot demand of his mouth softened until his lips were sliding against hers in soothing, gentle swipes. He finally lifted his head and after a long heated moment breathed hoarsely, "God... Frankie, look at you." His breath escaped in an explosive rush, as though he was struggling to contain his emotions.

A confused frown drew her brows together when she caught him staring at her with an expression she'd never seen before.

"Wh-what?" There was that stupid adolescent uncertainty again.

"You're beautiful," he murmured, kind of distracted but with more than a hint of annoyed wonder. "So beautiful...you take my breath away."

"I thought—" She broke off to swallow past the emotion clawing at her throat. "I thought you didn't like redheads?"

The question momentarily distracted him from

examining the shoulder he'd managed to reveal in the wide neckline of her T-shirt. He shook his head.

"I never said that."

"You did. I was seven and you said red hair was the sign of the devil."

He had the audacity to laugh at her disgruntled tone. "I was twelve," he said, as though that explained everything. "Besides, you'd probably done something annoying or reckless."

Okay, so maybe Frankie had made it her mission in life to annoy Nate, Jack and Ty because it had been the only time they'd paid any attention to her.

"And now?" she said softly.

His mouth curved into a sinful smile that would have melted her bones if she hadn't already been lying flat on her back in a puddle of lust.

He slid his hand up under her shirt and cupped her breast. "Can't you feel how annoyed I am?"

The sensation of his warm hand cupping her aching flesh had a moan sliding right up her throat. It also had her nipple tightening into a painful bud and she bit her lip.

Nate hummed with pleasure and shoved up

her top to watch his thumb brushing the pebbled peak. Both the look on his face and the feel of rough skin on hers had waves of pleasure and impatience rolling through her. Before she could ask if he intended to take his sweet time, he growled, "Look at you…all grown up and finally mi—" He broke off abruptly and rose to his knees, his rough hungry growl kind of thrilling.

"I wish you could see yourself," he said hoarsely, making her belly jump because she'd caught sight of something in his eyes, something she didn't normally see when Nate looked at her—desire…raw and naked and hot.

Her breath whooshed out. If she didn't have him in the next five minutes she would explode—all by herself.

Planting her socked foot against his chest, she purred, "Need any help, Commander Big Shot?" and gave a not-so-gentle shove. Nate slid off her sock in one impatient move, his smile sending her temperature soaring, then the other. He stilled when he caught sight of her bandages and he kissed her feet with a gentleness that had her throat tightening.

Nate's eyes glittered as he let his gaze slide up

the inside of her leg, pause and then take in her naked breasts and the flush of arousal making her skin glow. She shivered when he dropped a gentle kiss on her hip bone. Then, cupping her bottom, he leaned forward and kissed the tip of one breast as he whipped off her shorts. Finally, he leaned over her, hands planted either side of her head.

Frankie should have felt a little threatened by his size—by the latent power in the big body caging hers. The truth was she wanted him closer. Much...much...closer.

She slid her hands up his arms, ropey and tough with muscle, and curved them over his shoulders, her fingers soothing the teeth marks clearly visible beneath the satin-smooth tanned skin. Then she not-so-gently scored her nails down over his pecs, unable to prevent a tiny smile of triumph at his sharp inhalation.

"I've heard that SEALs are all talk and no action," she taunted softly, but Nate just chuckled as though no one would believe such a claim. A little annoyed by his arrogance—and, she had to admit, more than a little excited—Frankie shoved at his shoulders.

"All right, Commander Big Shot. Why don't you put your money where your big mouth is?" Her lips curved in a challenging smile. "Words are meaningless if you can't back them up with action."

One moment his breath escaped on a laugh, the next he'd made himself at home…right between her thighs.

Bending her knees, Frankie felt her eyes cross as the long, hard length of him slid against the tiny bundle of nerves right at her damp center. She caught her breath and bit down on her lip to prevent a moan from escaping.

"Fine by me, babe." He grinned, knowing—*the jerk*—exactly what he was doing to her. She must have been doing something to him too because he drew in air before dropping a quick kiss on her mouth. Then he rolled his hips and through the explosion inside her skull she thought she heard him murmur, "But I warn you… SEALs take no prisoners."

And then Frankie got lost somewhere between having her mouth possessed and her breasts ravished. She moaned through the torture of his lips sliding slowly down to her belly button, whimpered when he nibbled at the insides of her thighs, and gasped—her fingers clutching the sheets—when he took her in his mouth.

She came embarrassingly fast and then came a second time, almost as quickly and only just a little less violently. Flushed and panting, and eager for the feel of him inside her, she reached out to wrap her hand around him, but he growled. "Keep that up," he rasped hoarsely. "And it'll be all over."

With impatience he ripped the condom package with his teeth and fitted the latex to the bulging tip of his shaft with shaking hands.

She tried to help but he caught her hands and slid his fingers through hers. Then he crushed her mouth in a kiss that meant to consume...and thrust deep.

Surprise had Frankie jolting, her inner muscles tightening at the sudden invasion. Muttering a low curse, Nate stilled, his body hard and tense as though he was exercising enormous control. Through clenched teeth he bit out, "Francis? *You* okay?"

Shifting to relieve the slight discomfort—*he was a big guy*—Frankie bit her lip to keep from wincing. "It's…it's been a long time," she managed weakly.

He was silent a long moment before huffing out a low laugh. "Yeah. Me too… But don't worry," he promised softly, thrusting home when he felt her inner muscles relax to accommodate his size, "I think I can remember what to do next."

And then he proceeded to show her that he did indeed know what to do. In fact, when she came with him buried deep inside her body, it was so spectacular that she lost herself there for a moment…or five.

And she might even have heard herself cry out. Maybe.

And when he crushed her close and followed her over, his breath escaping in a long low groan of completion, Frankie thought very briefly that this…this was what she'd been waiting for her entire life. But then her thoughts slid away and all she could do was feel the heat and strength that surrounded her.

Seconds, minutes or hours later, Nate finally stirred. Realizing that she was wrapped around him like cling wrap, Frankie loosened her grip and took her first breath.

*Wow…*but that had been…*wow.* Words seemed inadequate to describe what had just happened and she needed a moment to gather herself because it had impacted her far more emotionally than a simple physical release was supposed to.

He'd touched something deep inside that was beginning to unfurl—and it scared her.

The trick here is to distance yourself, she lectured silently. *Hide your emotions…before he sees how much it meant to you.*

Fortunately, Frankie had had plenty of experience with that. Opening her eyes, she was a little unnerved to find him closer than was comfortable, studying her with an expression that had her belly instantly clenching.

The breath she'd just taken whooshed out. "Um, sorry." Even before the words were out, her brow tightened. *What the heck was she apologizing for?*

Annoyed, more with herself than him, she shoved at him and sat up when he finally rolled aside. Turning away, she pushed her hair off her face and noticed that her hands were shaking. "I guess…" She hid a grimace and casually reached for the sheet, suddenly feeling more vulnerable and exposed than she liked to admit. "I guess I got a little carried away."

Sprawled beside her and looking like he'd conquered the world—or maybe just hers—Nate folded his hands beneath his head, his mouth curving in a sensual smile as he continued to study her.

"I liked it."

"You…um, did?" she asked, before she could censor herself. Since when did she get all girly and insecure after a bout of hot, spectacular sex?

Nate gave a rough laugh and sat up, thrusting his fingers through his tousled hair. Hair she remembered clutching as her world spun completely out of control. He dropped a quick kiss on her exposed shoulder and rose. "Give me a couple of minutes," he growled in a sex-rough voice that had her inner muscles clenching. "And I'll prove exactly how much."

Struggling for nonchalance she was far from feeling, she picked at a loose thread, looking anywhere but at the sight of him disappearing into the bathroom.

Okay, so she totally watched his hard buns flex as he moved across the floor. Partly because he had a world-class ass…all high and tight with those little dents on the side, but mostly because she'd half expected him to dress and leave.

"Are you sure you can do that again, Nate?" she asked, sounding skeptical. There was a moment of silence before he reached out to curl one large tanned hand around the door frame. He slowly turned his head and Frankie could see by his stunned expression that no one had ever thought to question his stamina before.

"I mean, you're, what, thirty-five?"

For a long moment Nate studied her with an unreadable expression before he turned and disappeared into the bathroom.

Stifling a giggle, Frankie rolled onto her back and allowed her eyes to drift closed. She could practically feel the waves of outraged masculinity coming from the bathroom.

There was absolute silence for a couple of beats then the air changed subtly and she opened her eyes to see a spectacularly naked Nate standing beside the bed, staring down at her with hungry heat and a wicked smile.

Trying for confidence she was far from feeling, Frankie let her gaze wander down his impressively sculpted chest and abdomen to another impressive feature.

"You were saying?" he taunted softly, looking so pleased with himself that Frankie pretended to yawn. "Big deal," she murmured, closing her eyes. "Talk is cheap."

In the next instant she was flipped over onto her belly as though she weighed nothing more than a pancake. She gave a startled yelp and before she could laugh or demand to know what he thought he was doing, Nate had given her backside a smart slap and hauled her up onto her knees before him.

"Never let it be said," he murmured softly before giving her shoulder a punishing nip, "that a SEAL couldn't rise to the challenge."

Despite the stars exploding behind her eyes and the excitement gathering in the pit of her belly, Frankie laughed. "Actions," she teased again breathlessly, "speak louder than words."

His deep chuckle vibrated in his chest, sending tingles erupting across her sensitized flesh, and when he moved his lips from her shoulder to her ear, a shudder of excitement began as a deep humming in her core.

"It's a good thing, then," he murmured in a voice that made her body melt and her mind slip away, "that I'm a man of action, isn't it?"

CHAPTER TEN

JUST BEFORE DAWN, Nate carefully rose from the bed and scooped his pants off the floor as he headed for the door. His intention was to leave before Frankie, sprawled facedown across the bed in careless naked splendor, awakened, but it took all his SEAL discipline not to slide back against that warm, curvy body for another bout of spectacular sex.

And it had been spectacular. In fact, he couldn't ever remember sex being that good, but she needed her sleep and he needed a change of clothes as well as a shower before he headed off to work.

But it wasn't just work that drove him from her room without a backward glance. It was a desperate need to get away before she wormed her way any deeper under his skin.

Oh, yeah. And then there was the promise he'd made to his best friend. He wasn't sure "looking out for her" meant doing it up close and personal. During the past six hours, he'd conveniently forgotten that and hated what that said about him—that it was possible he was more like his father than he cared to admit.

Ignoring the pain in his side, Nate paused on the landing to pull on his still-damp uniform pants over his bed-warmed flesh. If the worst he suffered was a cold, wet ass, then he'd got off lightly because he'd spent the last thirty-five years trying to distance himself from his father's legacy and had no intention of starting to act like the man now. He'd taken advantage of someone he'd known his whole life, someone who trusted him, someone who'd been like a sister.

And he couldn't take it back.

That she'd taken advantage of him too—spectacularly—was beside the point. She didn't know about The Promise and she didn't know how much keeping that promise meant to him. Besides, he had enough responsibility in his life and should have known that coming here was a bad idea. But the sight of her standing on her front porch, looking like an Amazon princess on a war raid had floored him. He'd kind of lost his mind, ignored the little voice in his head warning him that he would only find trouble here.

The kind of trouble he was facing now. The kind a man found himself in when he discovered that his wild night had been more than just sex. More than a release of tension. What that more was exactly wasn't quite clear. What was clear, however, was the need for space.

But even as Nate scooped his damp blood-stained shirts off the entrance floor and quietly let himself out of the house, he knew he running. From the past few hours and from the fact that what he felt for Frankie might be more than he'd bargained for.

From the darkened window, Frankie watched a shirtless Nate pause and look up over his shoulder. And though there was no way he could see her, she froze, holding her breath, the hand clutching the sheet between her breasts tightening until her knuckles ached.

Light from the streetlamp poured over his tall, muscled frame, gilding half his body and face while leaving the other in total darkness. Even from this distance she could tell his expression was all hard lines and angular planes, unsoftened by any hint of a smile—by any hint of emotion—his posture all but screaming a remoteness, a distance she wished she could breach.

For some reason he wasn't ever going to let her in. The realization left a pinch in the region of her heart and Frankie spun away to sink back against the wall. Squeezing her eyes shut, she told herself that she wouldn't watch him leave. Not again.

Yet her ears strained for the sound of his truck and when it eventually came, the well-tuned purr competed with the rush of blood in her ears.

After it faded, she let out the breath she was still holding and pushed away from the wall. She absolutely did not care that he'd sneaked out without a *Thanks* or a *See ya around* as though she meant nothing to him but a couple of orgasms.

But that was fine, she told herself fiercely. At least he'd saved her from having to throw him out because she was done with him too. He'd given her exactly what she'd needed and had left before he could annoy her with his big body and bossy attitude. Great. Good. She hated sharing her space almost as much as she hated bossy alpha males.

Ignoring the little voice in the back of her mind calling her a liar, Frankie firmed her jaw and headed back to the bed, determined to get a couple more hours' sleep even if it killed her. But when she approached the rumpled covers and spotted the foil packets scattered across the floor, the thought of sliding back between sheets that smelled of him was suddenly more than she could face.

Because what had been an impulse brought on by heightened emotions had become so much more.

With a growl that sounded suspiciously like a sob she dropped the sheet she was still clutching like a lifeline and reached for a clean over-size T-shirt.

Emotions locked firmly away, she pulled it over her still-tingling flesh and stripped the bed, ripping everything off before stomping downstairs to dump the whole lot in the washing machine.

She added washing powder, set the program to sterilization and then headed upstairs to sterilize her body and scrub away the memory of the past five hours.

It was still dark when she left the house and set off on foot, her wallet and car keys tucked into her pockets as she headed for the hospital five miles away where her car was still parked.

She needed to do something or else she would go insane, and after being cooped up the past week she had a desperate need to head up the coast—to get out of Port St. John's.

She knew—from experience—that she couldn't outrun herself. But, hey, she would give it a darn good try.

It felt good to be in the crisp predawn air and Frankie sucked in deep lungs full of cool air redolent with salt and hints of the dark nearby forests. Walking at a fast clip, she ignored her still tender feet and willed her mind blank because that was the only way she was going to handle this.

Yet even the full force of her will couldn't lock away images of the past few hours. Images of Nate's hot gaze holding hers as he drove her out of her mind with pleasure. Of the rough scrape of his jaw against her sensitized flesh…of the heavy weight of his body as he uttered a long low moan and collapsed over her, breathing roughly, heart thundering, muscles twitching in the aftermath.

You got me into this mess, she told her body furiously when her good parts tingled and melted. *You should have let me kick his ass instead of exploring all those yummy muscles with my hands and mouth before licking him from head to toe.*

Arrrgh. Pressing her fist against the pressure in her chest, Frankie told herself she didn't need all the conflicting signals he constantly sent out and she certainly didn't need his bossy, annoying attitude. She didn't *need* anyone. Least of all a man who'd ignored her for the past twelve years, pretended she didn't exist the months he'd been home, and then stormed back into her life, thinking he could order her around.

Nope, she didn't need him.

Want, however, was something else entirely. Something her body was all too eager to remind her of. And her mind…well, it seemed just as rebellious as her stupid body.

Fine. She wanted him. Big deal. He was pretty to look at and he had some awesome skills in the bedroom. But it was over now and she—and her body—could just get over themselves. They'd had him and once had been enough.

More than enough.

But even as she thought it, a growing feeling of misery lodged like a hot ball of lead in her chest. As for her heart, well, its job was to pump blood around her body and that was all. It had no business yearning for things that would never be. *She* would never be the kind of woman Nate wanted.

A few days after the biggest mistake of his adult life, Nate caught sight of Frankie walking out of the ER ambulance bay looking like a warrior goddess in the dark blue EMT jumpsuit. She'd immediately caught his attention—along with that of just about every other guy in the car park, including the rookies he was escorting to get their routine shots because their medic hadn't yet been replaced after his unexpected heart attack.

With her head thrown back as she laughed at something the young guy she was with said, she looked more carefree than he'd ever seen, but it was the overly familiar body language of the other man that roused some very dark, very alien emotions in Nate's gut. Especially as Frankie seemed to be enjoying the closeness—a little too much for a woman who just a few days ago had been all over *him* like he was the frosting on a huge piece of chocolate cake and she was ravenous.

His mind instantly conjured up images of Frankie and the guy that had his teeth practically cracking under the strain of his clenched jaw. Oblivious to the tension humming through his body, the rookies had completely embarrassed themselves and the uniform by letting out a couple of wolf whistles.

Frankie had instantly turned her head and her eyes had locked with his for a couple of beats— no smile of recognition in their leafy-green depths. But even as he'd felt his heart rate speed up and his mouth begin to curl into an involuntary smile, she'd turned and walked away; without acknowledging him in any way other than that one brief unreadable glance. Without a sign that just a few nights ago he'd rocked her world.

Without even a *Hey, keep your pets in check* quip he'd half expected.

And as he watched her slender back and swaying hips disappear, he was tempted to follow and punch the guy before grabbing her and pushing her up against the nearest wall. He wanted to kiss her—remind her of the other night—until her eyes went soft with arousal and she made that little hitching noise in her throat that drove him wild.

The fact that he'd been at the hospital in his official capacity and that he was back on his promise wagon stopped him. Oh, yeah, and the fact that she'd think he'd lost his mind and have him committed.

And even if he'd felt as though he had, Nate Oliver was an ex-Navy SEAL. SEALs completed their mission—no matter what.

And his mission: to honor a promise to a dead man.

But although Nate had tried, going back to the way things had been was more difficult than he'd anticipated. He might have washed her scent from his skin but no amount of scrubbing could rid him of the feeling that he'd messed up. Watching her climax had been the hottest, most erotic experience of his life, and if he'd wondered why it had happened with Frankie of all people, he was going to ignore it because dealing with her had always been like negotiating a minefield. One misstep and everything could blow up in his face.

In one thing she *was* predictable, though, he mused wryly. She was *un*predictable, and in the days that followed he found himself tensing every time his phone rang or chimed an incoming message. But Frankie never called or texted. In fact, she seemed completely unfazed by something that had rocked him to his emotional foundation: that their night had been more than a quick release after months of abstinence.

He'd heard that she'd been partying it up at the Seafarers and what he experienced could only be described as jealousy. It was an emotion he'd *never* once felt when it came to women. And he didn't like it.

Not one little bit.

CHAPTER ELEVEN

IT WAS TOWARD the end of the following week that Nate admitted he was in serious trouble. First he zoned out during a meeting and then he nearly passed out on a routine swimming exercise, drawing a concerned reprimand from the base commander and orders to get himself checked out.

Since the base medic had still not been replaced, Nate was ordered to go to the ER for a checkup. He didn't need a doctor to tell him that his wound was infected but since it would only be fixed by a course of antibiotics and expert wound care, he simply nodded and left the base. No way would he make the mistake of going to Frankie, though. Not after what had happened the last time.

Sighing, he drove to the hospital, hoping he wouldn't see the redhead currently making his life a living hell.

Prepared for a long wait, he was surprised to find the ER relatively quiet as he headed for the admissions counter. The nurse who'd been on duty the night of the fire looked up as he approached.

She straightened her navy shirt and batted her eyelashes in such a blatant attempt at flirting that Nate smiled, despite the pain and fever racking his body. "Here to let me make your dreams come true, sailor?" she asked boldly.

He managed a chuckle and a pointed glance at her wedding band before rasping, "Since you're already married, my dreams will have to remain unfulfilled."

"Your loss." She laughed. "So, what can I help you with, handsome?"

Nate seriously thought about leaving, but reluctantly admitted, "I need to see a doctor."

Her gaze sharpened and she must have seen something in his face because she instantly came round the counter to take his arm. "Let's get you into one of the bays and I'll find you one."

Unwilling to admit just how wobbly he felt, Nate shook his head and locked his knees. "I'll wait here."

After a long searching look, the nurse disappeared, leaving Nate to lean against the counter as a wave of prickly heat and dizziness washed over him. The next thing he knew someone was calling his name and shaking his arm.

"Nate? Nate, what's wrong? Can you hear me?"

He cracked open his eyes and Paige's concerned face swam into view. "Nate, are you sick?"

Embarrassed by the display of weakness, he quickly straightened and scrubbed a hand over his face, hoping to clear his head. One minute he was hot and feverish, the next racked with sweaty chills. He'd felt this way only once before in his life, when he'd been in the field, nursing a gunshot wound.

Abruptly aware of their curious audience, Nate lowered his voice. "Can we have some privacy, Doc?" he rasped. "I need…um…" Swaying, he sucked in air and admitted quickly, "I need medical assistance."

Paige's eyes widened and quickly flashed over him, probably expecting to see blood. Seeing none, she grabbed his hand and steered him toward the swing doors. "Nancy, which bay is clean?" she called out, practically dragging him along like she was afraid he'd bolt.

Another nurse popped her head out a doorway and straightened when she saw Nate. "Bay Seven is clear. Dr. Reyes is on his way."

"All right. It's okay, Nate, we've got you," she said, shoving Nate ahead of her into the unoccupied bay. As she drew the curtains she demanded, "It's the gunshot wound, isn't it?"

Frankie pulled the ambulance up to the emergency entrance and shoved the vehicle into park before hopping out and hurrying to the rear. Her partner, Dale Franklin, was ready with the collapsible gurney, jumping down the instant she opened the doors.

Grabbing the ventilation bag with one hand and using the other to assist with the dismount, she quickly checked the mobile heart monitor, cursing when she realized their patient was crashing again. It had been like this since they'd arrived at the scene.

She yelled, "He's crashing again," as she and Dale took off through the doors. "High-voltage burns to hands and arms. ACLS protocols observed, patient unresponsive and intubated on signs of respiratory muscle paralysis. Fourth-degree burns to right hand, third and second degree to left hand and both forearms. Possible fractures to phalanges and ulna."

Dale added, "Catheter inserted with no immediate signs of MGB. Kidney function appears to be coping with increased fluid treatment."

"Cranial and spinal injuries?" Dr. Thornton demanded, striding down the passage toward them as they rushed the patient into the trauma bay.

"He was thrown over twenty feet in an explosion and appears to have a lump on the back of his head," Frankie reported. "Pupil reflex is normal at this stage but I'm more concerned with tetanic injuries and damage to his heart. We've struggled to keep him stable."

The next fifteen minutes were spent in controlled chaos and shouted instructions. Frankie assisted in the transfer, answering the terse questions quickly and concisely.

They'd arrived on the scene where the patient and his partner had been conducting routine maintenance on the city's main power supply. As far as she could tell, something had gone wrong with the safety switch, resulting in an arc explosion. It wasn't clear why he hadn't been wearing his safety gloves and if his hands had been damp, but he'd been thrown twenty feet in the explosion. His partner had immediately run to his aid and started CPR until other personnel had arrived on the scene. They had cut the smoking coverall fabric away from his hands, which were a mangled mess of burnt flesh and damaged tissue.

He'd been covered with a space blanket and his burned hands wrapped in sections of cut-up space blanket to await the EMS.

Immediately on arrival, Frankie and Dale had activated ACLS, or advanced cardio-life support, and intubated him at signs of respiratory paralysis. They'd then removed the rest of his coveralls to assess the damage, inserting a saphenous IV in his groin instead of a PICC in order to bypass the injured arms and exit wounds on his feet.

Once they'd fitted a neck brace they'd moved him to a spinal board and performed a twelve-lead ECG. He'd gone into cardiac arrest twice, forcing them to use the paddles.

Once Dale could handle him on his own, Frankie—having more advanced driver training—had taken the wheel.

After returning the equipment to the ambulance and submitting their procedure report to the ER staff, Frankie headed toward the EMS offices, wishing she didn't have a ton of paperwork to get through. It had been a really busy afternoon and she was tired, hungry and needed a shower in the worst way.

She also hadn't been sleeping lately and blamed the heat wave for it because no way would she admit that *he* was responsible. No way would she admit that the minute she closed her eyes she relived that night over and over and over again until she wanted to scream with frustration that was as much temper as sexual frustration.

She spotted Dale heading toward her, carrying a two-cup tray and stuffing his face with a Boston cream donut. Another donut was perched on top of the cup he held out to her.

She took the cup and tossed him the donut. "How many times do I have to tell you these things will kill you? They're loaded with sugar, GMOs and trans fats. You're better off eating cardboard."

"Yeah, yeah," he mumbled, licking cream off his lip as he bit into the second donut. "My liver appreciates your concern but even with my diet of champions I'm likely to live a long life. Even if it's just to watch you get all bent outta shape over your boyfriend."

Not willing to discuss her pitiful love life and sound even lamer than she was, Frankie snorted, stepped around him and continued walking. She should have known that Dale wouldn't take the hint, and within seconds he'd caught up with her.

"An interesting reaction there, Ms. Bryce."

"Not that interesting," she said dryly. "Considering I don't have a boyfriend." No one knew about Nate or that night and although Paige suspected, she didn't know for sure. Frankie was all too happy to pretend nothing had happened.

"That's not what I hear," he said, casually chewing on the greasy pastry and sending her a curious sideways glance.

"Yeah, well, maybe you shouldn't believe everything you hear." She lowered her voice. "Besides, the only reason I let people think it's true is to get rid of guys like that," she added, nodding as the new EMT, Hank, pushed his way through the ER doors.

"New guy been making a nuisance of himself?"

Frankie lifted her coffee to her mouth, making a humming sound of agreement.

"Want me to beat him up?" Dale demanded out loud when, sure enough, the other man swaggered up.

"No." Frankie chuckled and nudged his shoulder affectionately. "But you know you're my hero, right?"

"What about me?" Hank demanded with a smirk that often made Frankie want to smack him. "Am I your hero too?"

"There's only place for one in my life," she said smoothly. "And that's my partner."

Hank sent Dale a dismissive glance before turning back to Frankie. "Seems like a henpecked husband to me," he snorted. "If not me, then what about that coastie guy I hear you're dating?"

"Now, there's a *real* hero," her partner piped up smugly. "He's an ex-SEAL and probably knows a hundred ways to kill a man and make it look like a natural death."

"People talk about those guys as though they're superheroes," Hank argued, getting a little red in the face. "But I know for a fact that your guy isn't bulletproof."

Frankie stiffened. "What does that mean?"

"I'm talking about the fact that he's been shot." He laughed. "I heard he even fainted."

For a moment Frankie's breath froze in her throat. Her heart lurched in her chest before settling down into a ragged rhythm. "That was last week," she said as casually as she could, a tremble of relief escaping along with her exhalation. "And he didn't faint or even pass out then so I can't see him doing it now."

Dale's eyes widened and he quickly grabbed the donut out of his mouth before it fell.

"He got shot? For real?"

She shrugged. "It was just a flesh wound." He'd come around for some first aid, stayed long enough to rock her world before leaving without saying goodbye, *Thanks for rocking my world* or even a *See ya around, babe*.

He seemed to have forgotten everything about

her, including where she lived, a point he'd hammered home by not calling, texting or even sending a message in a bottle.

Frankie was smart enough to know what that meant. He was done with her now that he'd done her. *Jerk*.

"Hmm."

Hank's smirk was enough to draw an impatient "What?" from Frankie, in a tone that usually sent people running. But it seemed the other man's ego kept him from picking up on verbal cues because, instead of backing off, he said, "Just that maybe he isn't as invincible as you think. Lieutenant Thinks-he's-a-Badass is in Bay Seven, being fawned over by a bunch of nurses. Your friend Paige is there too, looking suitably concerned."

What? Nate was here? Frankie's blood ran cold then hot then cold again.

"It's Lieutenant *Commander*," she snapped. "Why the hell can't people remember something as simple as a man's rank?" And before the two men could do anything more than gape at her, Frankie spun on her heel and headed for the ER.

She would not to lose it, she told herself, because losing it meant she cared. And why would she care about someone who thought so little of *her*?

But she did care, she thought as a strangled sob caught in her throat. More than she wanted to. And the news that he was in the ER, hurt and possibly bleeding to death, had Frankie flying down the passage toward the ER bays, her stomach a ball of dread, her nerves jittering like she'd guzzled a gallon of coffee.

She reached Bay Seven and whipped aside the curtain, only to find it empty.

Spinning in a fast circle, she spied an intern lounging at the nurses' station and called out, "The guy in Seven. Have you seen him?"

"The gunshot guy?" He looked up with an absent frown. "Gone."

She halted in her tracks as his words sank in. *Gone.* There was a buzzing in her ears and her world abruptly tilted on its axis. "Gone?"

"Yeah. Departed." He must have seen something in her face because he shot to his feet. "I mean not gone gone," he hurriedly explained. "He left on his own two feet."

The pressure around her forehead eased. "And you didn't stop him?"

He gaped at her. "You're kidding, right? That guy is built like a cyborg. Besides, he was looking…" he narrowed his eyes at her "…kinda like you're looking right now. Scary. Are you okay?"

"What about the attending physician?" she demanded, barely resisting the urge to head over there and throttle him for making her think that Nate was…well, gone. Permanently.

The intern shrugged apologetically and went back to whatever he'd been doing before she'd interrupted him.

Feeling as though her brain was about to explode, Frankie took another look into the empty bay and decided that since there were no signs of blood, Nate was most likely in one piece.

She expelled the breath she'd been holding. He was okay. He was alive and walking. "Men are stupid," she muttered to herself, wondering how long ago he'd left and if she would find him passed out in the car park.

A dry feminine voice said behind her, "You won't get any argument from me," and Frankie spun around to see an ER nurse pushing a teenager in a wheelchair. He was bruised, bloodied and was hugging both his left arm and a battered skateboard to his skinny chest.

"Alpha flip or pop shuvit?" she asked, hoping to calm her crazy before she found Nate.

The kid's torn lip curled. "Those are for little kids," he scoffed. "I was trying the new hospital flip."

"Guess you tanked it, huh?"

He looked a little sheepish as Nancy shook her head and rolled him into an open bay.

Frankie headed down the passage to the nearest exit and pulled out her phone to call Nate. It went directly to voice mail and with a muttered curse she shoved it into her back pocket just as she rounded a corner and nearly collided with Paige.

"Frankie, did you hear—"

"Yep, and now he's not answering his phone." She lifted a hand to the headache blooming into life behind her right eye.

"I'm sorry. I offered to drive him," Paige admitted, "but he acted like I'd insulted his manhood and stomped off."

"Idiots," Frankie muttered, and rubbed her forehead. "Men are such idiots."

Paige sighed her agreement. "But we still love them, right?"

"Right," Frankie said dryly, before expelling her breath in a loud whoosh. *Not going there*, she thought. "Maybe I should go make sure the big oaf doesn't wrap himself around a tree."

"Need some help?"

Frankie snorted and strode toward the exit, pretending she wasn't in a hurry. "Please, like I can't handle an idiot guy with my hands tied behind my back."

"You sound just like him, do you know that?" Paige called out, making Frankie feel just a little insulted.

"*I* am not the idiot that left after passing out in the ER. I just don't want any witnesses when I kill *him* for being one."

"Good luck with that," Paige snorted. "There's an entire race of males you'll have to take on."

No, there wasn't, Frankie fumed as she hurried down the ramp toward employee parking. After she'd checked—because that's what friends did—that he hadn't passed out behind the wheel of his brand-new truck and smashed into a tree or driven over a cliff, she was done with men. Finished. Kaput.

Especially the ones with hero complexes. The ones who kissed you like you were the missing piece of their soul, like they wanted to consume you one kiss, one greedy bite at a time, gave you a few mind-blowing orgasms—then left without a single word.

Oh, yeah, she was done.

For the rest of freaking eternity.

CHAPTER TWELVE

THE SUN WAS dipping low on the horizon when Frankie turned west and headed along the coastal road to Rocky Bay, creatively named because of the many rocks littering the cove. She'd never been to Nate's house, but knew from Terri that he'd bought a fixer-upper overlooking the small bay.

Turning off Ocean Drive, Frankie had only gone a couple of hundred yards when she came across Nate's truck, abandoned on the side of the road a good half-mile from his house.

Chest abruptly squeezing, she pulled in behind the truck and shoved her car into park before hopping out to check—half expecting to find glass, crumpled metal and a bleeding unconscious alpha.

She found the vehicle empty and allowed her breath to escape in a loud whoosh. Okay, so no crumpled metal and no unconscious alpha...

which was good. Also good, she decided when she tried the door, was the discovery that it was locked. It meant Nate couldn't have been too out of it if he'd remembered to lock his precious truck. But then again he was a guy, and guys tended to treat their vehicles better than they treated people.

She tried his phone and heard ringing coming from inside the cab. Cursing, she got back into her car and shoved it into gear. Driving slowly, she craned her neck and squinted into the deepening shadows on both sides of the road for any sign that he'd wandered off and passed out in someone's yard.

Or fallen into a ditch.

Houses on this side of town were spaced further apart and the forest tended to encroach, which was why she missed Nate's road and had to reverse before finally locating Gull's Way. Bouncing over the rough spots, she totally understood why he'd bought the truck.

His house was at the end of the beach access lane, a sprawling log cabin that in the gathering gloom looked like it had been neglected but showed recent signs of renovation.

Light spilled from the neighboring houses but number eight Gull's Way was in darkness—a fact that set her nerves jangling because it meant he hadn't made it home.

Where was he?

Working to not go into a total freak-out, she sat, thumbs tapping the steering wheel and nerves jittering at the image of him taking the stairs built into the side of the cliff and tumbling down onto the rocky beach fifty feet below.

Her breath backed up in her throat. Or…what if he'd gone onto the front deck, fainted again and fallen over the railing? What if—

"Stop already," she snapped, swallowing her heart, which had lodged in her stupid throat. The words, spoken aloud, settled her and she turned into his driveway and pulled up a few yards from the wooden porch.

She shoved the vehicle into park, telling herself that the wide open front door didn't mean that his place had been burgled and she wasn't about to walk into a crime scene. It just meant she'd been watching way too many cop shows on TV. Port St. John's still had that small-town feel and people rarely locked their doors. Besides, bad guys had most likely heard that Nate was an even badder guy than they were and were keeping away.

Shaking her head at the idiocy of the male species, Frankie grabbed her phone and got out, then took the stairs and stepped over the threshold into the dark house.

"Nate?"

In the ambient light, she could see very little in the way of furniture, as if he hadn't bothered to decorate the place. But when she ventured in a little further and caught sight of a sawhorse, piles of planks and machine tools, she was reminded of all the DIY scenes she'd been called to because guys thought that having a Y chromosome meant they could use power tools without reading the safety instructions.

What if…?

Stop it, she ordered silently. *He's fine. He's an ex-Navy SEAL, for God's sake, and…and he'd better be fine.*

Or she was going to kill him herself.

"Nathan?"

Being greeted by further silence, Frankie did a quick tour of the living room, kitchen, study—which had been turned into a home gym—and headed down the short passage to the master bedroom. Half expecting to find him passed out on his bed, she was surprised—and more than a little concerned—to find it not only empty but as neat as a pin.

Beginning to panic, because it seemed more and more likely that something bad had happened to him, Frankie retraced her steps. She was just about to call 911 when she heard a soft sound coming from the deck. She whipped her head toward it and noticed that the French doors were standing open.

The newly built deck was in darkness when she stepped out and looked around before heading for the flimsy makeshift railing. Carefully peering over the side, she hoped she'd be able to see him if he'd fallen over the edge…but equally praying that she wouldn't see anything but rocks.

The sun had by now dropped into the sea and she could see…absolutely nothing. She gritted her teeth. It meant she'd have to get her flashlight and do a little night recon. Muttering to herself about stupid alpha guys and their stupid big egos, Frankie turned to retrace her steps when a deep, rough bedroom voice growled, "Get away from the damn edge," nearly giving her a coronary.

She gave a startled yelp and stumbled backward—right into those flimsy bits of wood. There was an ominous crack as a plank abruptly gave way behind her. She opened her mouth to gasp, *"Seriously?"* and tried to grab onto something solid, but her heel caught the edge of some planks and she felt herself begin to fall.

She had a flashback to the night of the storm, thought, *Well, this sucks*...fully expecting to go tumbling backward onto the rocks below when hard fingers closed around her wrist and she was yanked forward against a hard body with enough force to knock the breath from her lungs.

"Oomph," she said.

At the same time an irritated male voice snarled, *"What the hell, woman?"*

Adrenaline flashing through her at warp speed, Frankie clung to the only solitary, steady, solid thing in a dangerously unstable world. Then again Nate had always been a rock—a really big, hard, yummy rock. A rock whose heart was pounding almost as hard as hers and muttering curses that ended with, "It's a full-time job keeping you out of trouble."

Reminded that she was giving up men permanently, Frankie snatched her hands off him and glared up into the achingly familiar face above hers. Only, instead of the hot sexy expression he'd been wearing the last time she'd been this close, he was scowling at her as though she was the last person he wanted to see.

Before she could stop it, hurt sliced through her and in reaction she shoved away from him… only to be roughly yanked back and forcefully removed from the edge of the deck. *"What's wrong with you?"* he growled roughly. "Do you have a death wish?"

Slapping at his hands, she gulped and gasped at the same time, which should have been impossible but totally wasn't. Realizing she was trembling—from relief at the near disaster, she told herself and not because he was warm and she was tempted to bury her face in his neck—Frankie planted her palms on his chest and shoved, aggravation ratcheting up a couple of notches when he remained as steady as a mountain.

Steady, when she felt as though she was floundering in quicksand.

He pulled back with a look that said she was crazy before saying, "You're welcome, by the way, for saving you." He sounded a little rough around the edges, like maybe the fact that she'd nearly died had affected him. But then she took in his tousled hair and the pillow crease on his cheek and realized he'd been napping.

Taking a freaking nap while she'd been on the verge of panicking.

He gave her a little shake and demanded, "You think I should have given you a nudge instead, Francis?"

Frankie realized in a blinding flash of awareness that he hadn't needed to give her a nudge at all. She sucked in a horrified breath as she realized that she'd gone and done what she'd promised herself she wouldn't.

She'd fallen. Flat on her face. All by herself.

Again. For the only man on the face of the planet to drive her completely crazy. Only this time it was no teenage crush.

She backed away, realizing this was the second stupidest thing she'd ever done. Actually, no, she amended. Falling for Nate was by far the stupidest thing she'd ever done because all she'd got for diving off Devil's Point other than the nickname Fearless Frankie had been a broken arm. This was…well, she'd be lucky to survive without a broken heart.

Something that was a lot harder to fix.

Furious—at herself more than him—Frankie spun away to stalk across the deck, breathing like she'd run up the north face of the Olympic mountains. She needed a moment—heck, she needed a whole bunch—and maybe to hide in the dark too, because that penetrating gaze always saw way too much.

Frankly, she'd rather throw herself off the deck than have him see what she'd only just discovered herself. Something that was as doomed now as it had been when she'd been a kid.

"What is wrong with you?" she demanded, momentarily unsure whether she was asking him or herself. Spinning around to face him again, she decided to handle him first. She'd deal with herself later.

And *then* there'd be hell to pay.

"You don't answer your phone. You abandon

your truck ten miles away and then when I get here your front door is wide open and you're nowhere to be found. I was about to call 911, thinking you'd fallen off your deck, you…you—"

"I felt a little queasy and decided to walk," he interrupted roughly, and Frankie was glad because she couldn't think of a bad enough name to call him. But he'd already lost interest in her, turning to inspect the broken railing and muttering something about "damn fool women"… or was that wo*man*, as in singular?

She yelped, "Excuse me? *I'm* not the idiot here. *You* are, thinking you're so tough and invincible."

Ignoring her, Nate grabbed a nearby plank and a discarded hammer and went to work repairing the rail. "What are you doing here, Frankie?" he demanded in a voice that was as tired as it was distant.

Momentarily distracted by the play of muscles in his back and arms, Frankie thought, *Okay, so he doesn't want to talk. Fine.* He could darn well listen—but it would have been nice if he'd at least pretend to be happy to see her.

"I heard you fainted at the hospital and then refused to let Paige drive yo—"

"I did not *faint*," he interrupted, straightening with a snap and sounding as though she'd just insulted his manhood. "Women faint, and even if Paige hadn't been busy I..." He lifted one hand to press a couple of fingers into his forehead like he had a headache. "Look, I don't need a babysitter, okay? I'm fine."

"And I *do*, is that what you're saying?"

His sigh sounded more than a little impatient. "All I'm saying is that I'm an adult. I don't need anyone checking up on me like I'm ten."

She snorted and stomped closer. "Right. That's why you left your truck on the side of the road? Because you're an adult?" His fleeting glance was unreadable before he dropped the hammer into the nearby toolbox.

Incensed by his air of masculine superiority, Frankie cocked one hip and shoved her hands on her hips to glare at him. "Oh, right, silly me. I forgot for a moment that SEALs are immune to the same weakness that occasionally afflicts the rest of humanity."

He nudged her away from the edge, put himself between her and the flimsy rail, then folded his arms across his mile-wide chest and stared down at her as though she was speaking Swahili.

"You're human, Nate," she snapped. "You hurt, you bleed. Not…" she poked his pec with her finger "…a cyborg. Or some stupid superhero dodging bullets or healing in the blink of an eye. Someone who should accept a hand from his friends once in a while, instead of thinking he's everyone else's self-appointed protector."

He arched a dark brow. "You wanna go there, princess?"

It was Frankie's turn to demand, "What is *that* supposed to mean?"

He sighed and squeezed the bridge of his nose. "Nothing. Look, I'm fine, okay? And for your information, I'm no hero." He gave a harsh laugh and folded his arms across his chest. "You, better than anyone, know exactly how *human* I am."

She opened her mouth to ask what he was talking about and shut it with a snap when he just arched a brow, clearly reminding her of the other night when he—

Face flaming, she sucked in a sharp breath, suddenly grateful for the darkness that hid her expression from those golden-brown eyes. Eyes that seemed to see everything yet gave nothing away.

"Aaargh," she growled in frustration. "Trust a stupid man to bring that up." She squeezed her head between her hands and turned away but then something occurred to her and she spun back round. "And since you did, let's talk about that, shall we?" She lowered her hands and scowled at him. "And the way you left. Sneaking out like I…" She swallowed an unpleasant notion. "Like I'm something you're ashamed of."

His expression abruptly closed down and his mouth firmed into a tight line of irritation, leaving him looking about as approachable as a grizzly. "Let's not."

"Fine," Frankie snapped, and before she could stop it, the implication that he *was* ashamed of her lodged like a sharp ache right beside her heart.

He must have seen something in her expression because he sighed and looked pained. "Frankie—"

"No, it's okay." She gave a shaky laugh and spun away. "I mean, it's not the first time I've disappointed someone—or you, for that matter.

And given my track record, it's not likely to be the last."

"It's not *you*. It's—"

She turned on him with a warning snarl. "Finish that and I'll gut you like a fish."

He sighed as though she was a huge pain in the butt. "Just drop it, okay?"

"Why? Because *you* said so?" She asked, annoyed with his calm inscrutability when she was certain steam was escaping from her ears. "Because you're an ex-Navy SEAL who can kill with a single blow?" Furious and hurting, she couldn't stop the words pouring out of her mouth. "Because 'heroes' don't need to have a reason or explain themselves to lesser mortals?"

He closed his hand over hers and the ease with which he managed to render her immobile had Frankie's simmering temper igniting.

"I thought..." She drew in a shuddery breath and yanked her hand away, surprised when Nate released her. She wrapped her arms around herself as though to protect herself from the memory of losing someone she cared about. She'd loved her brother and his death had hit her hard, but she knew losing Nate would devastate her.

"*We* were worried about you, Nate." *I was worried about you.*

"I'm fine." His tone was coolly dismissive, as was the way he folded his arms across his chest. "Look, it was a…mistake. I blame myself because it shouldn't have happened." Frankie blinked and opened her mouth to ask him what he was talking about when Nate continued. "You and I?" He waggled a long masculine finger between them. "Not going to happen again. Ever."

For a long moment Frankie stared up into his face—half-hidden in shadows—and felt herself go cold because she'd just realized something horrifying. Something so mortifying that it left her feeling exposed and raw…because somewhere buried deep she'd harbored the small, fragile hope that one day—

Oh, hell, no.

Swallowing past the burning lump of humiliation that lodged in her throat, she gave a short, ragged laugh. "You…you arrogant, self-important…*ass.*" Her reaction must have surprised him because a wrinkle appeared between his dark brows and he was suddenly looking at her like she was live ammo likely to go off any moment. "What makes you think *I* want a you and me?"

He didn't reply but one dark brow hiked up his forehead.

Infuriated, she gasped, "You're joking, right? *You...*" she jabbed a finger at him "...are the last man on earth that I'd want *any*thing with. The last man I'd *look* to for anything other than a few quick orgasms."

His expression hardened. "Why, because my father was the town loser who lied and cheated his way into every woman's bed? A man whose word meant about as much as his marriage vows?"

"What?" Frankie's mouth dropped open. "Have you lost your mind?"

He sighed and thrust an impatient hand through his hair, leaving it more rumpled than ever. "Maybe. But *my* word happens to mean something."

What? Frowning, Frankie curled her hands into tight fists and then folded her arms beneath her breasts when her fingers itched to smooth all that thick silky mess. She shook her head to clear it. "You're not making any sense. Have you been drinking?"

Hands shoved into his pockets, he turned to stare out at the bay. In the darkness, Frankie saw his jaw flex and for a long moment thought he wouldn't reply. Finally, he said quietly, unemotionally, "I made a promise."

Okay, so that wasn't what Frankie had expected. "A what?" She shook her head, confused. "I mean, to whom?"

He sent her a brief unreadable glance. "I promised Jack I'd look out for you."

She stared at him, more than a little stunned by the news. "J-Jack? Wha—"

Somehow Frankie had known this moment would come, when she would be forced to talk about Jack.

She stared at Nate, hoping for some sign of softening, but his profile might as well have been carved in granite. "The night before we shipped out that first time," he said flatly, "he made me swear that if anything ever happened to him, I'd look out for you."

"Seriously? I was a *kid* then, Nate, something I no longer am—in case you haven't noticed."

"I broke my promise to my best friend," he continued with quiet intensity. "A promise I swore to keep, no matter what."

"Jack's dead."

"Which is why I—"

"He's gone, Nate," she interrupted abruptly. "Gone, trying to be a damn hero."

"He *was* a hero," he said with quiet intensity.

Frankie sucked in the sharp edge of grief that threatened to overwhelm her and spun away. "Yes. And look where that got him."

He sighed, the sound heavy with apology, regret and his own grief. "I'm sorry."

"Yeah, me too." Sorry for so many things. "But I'm not thirteen anymore, Nate," she reminded him tersely. "I'm a big girl now. I have a job, pay all my own bills and manage to dress and feed myself every morning." She pressed shaking fingers to her temples, where a blinding headache had finally exploded into being. "Besides, the Jack I knew would hardly expect you to honor some silly adolescent pledge for all eternity."

"Then you didn't know your brother," he drawled in a tone that said she was being overly dramatic and difficult. "He meant it and so did I."

"Arrrgh!" Her frustration emerged as a growl.

"I don't *need* some *man* thinking I need a keeper and it's…it's insulting that you think I do."

"It doesn't matter what you think," he said quietly, implacably, confirming what Frankie was beginning to realize. Nate viewed her as one of his responsibilities.

Only she didn't need saving. She never had.

"I am *not* your responsibility, Nate," she snapped. "I'm no one's responsibility." Struggling to control her breathing, Frankie wondering if her hair was smoking because it felt like her brain was boiling inside her skull. "Who do you think you are?" she continued when she could form words.

"Frankie—"

"How dare you! What right do you have to assume responsibility for *me*?"

"Jack—"

"Don't you dare," she interrupted furiously. "Don't you dare add me to the rest of your responsibilities, Nate. In fact…" She blinked back tears and spun away from him, determined that he never know how much his words, his attitude tore at her. Never know that she felt as though she'd been gut shot.

Sucking in a shaky breath, she headed for the doors. "In fact, you can just write me off as a...a loser and forget you ever—"

Before she'd taken two steps, Frankie was spun around and slammed up against his hard body. She gave a surprised squeak that was instantly swallowed as his mouth covered hers in a kiss filled with such fury, frustration and wild need that she instinctively brought up her hands to soothe.

She had a moment to think, *What...?* before he growled, "And don't *you* dare call what we did 'just sex', Francis," he growled, pulling away and leaving her swaying at the abrupt assault on her senses.

"Go home, Frankie," he said quietly, wiping his hands down his face as though he was beyond weary and, without another word, turned to face the darkened bay—obviously done with the conversation.

Obviously done with her.

Hurt burrowed deep and for several beats she stared at his wide, tense shoulders, her heart squeezing at the image he presented. Big. Tough. Distant. As isolated as the mountain peaks he faced. A man alone, shouldering the burdens of everyone around him.

But he didn't have to and *she* didn't want to be a weight he carried on his shoulders. She was a strong, independent woman who could shoulder her own burdens—and maybe some of his.

She opened her mouth to tell him but another look at the implacable set of his shoulders told her that he'd never let her close enough to help. Never let her close enough to care.

"You know what I think, Nate?" she said after a short silence during which she struggled with her battered emotions. She had to swallow past what felt like a huge shard of glass in her throat. "I think you use that stupid promise to evade the real issue here." When he remained silent, she gave a tight laugh and continued, "For all your medals, for all your bravery and courage, you're a coward. Too scared to let yourself care, let yourself be vulnerable to anyone, because they might leave you like your father did. Like Jack and your team did. Well," she reminded him fiercely, "I'm *still* here."

His answer was a whole lot of silence that had Frankie flinging at his head, "But, then, I guess you think no one can function without you around to protect them. Even from themselves." The backs of her eyes stung and she swallowed the sob rising in her throat, threatening to cut off her breath and humiliate her.

She wouldn't cry. Not in front of him. In fact, he wasn't worth the swollen eyes, stuffy nose or blinding headache.

"Well, let me tell you something, Commander Big Shot," she said fiercely. "I survived just fine without your 'protection' for the last twelve years, and I'll survive the next fifty. So you can just scratch me off your Things-I-Have-to-Take-Care-Of list." Her throat finally closed as she spun on her heel and left before she broke down.

Broke down and begged him to love her.

At the French doors, she paused and sucked in a steadying breath. With one hand on the wooden frame, she looked back over her shoulder. Nate hadn't moved and the set of his wide shoulders was as tense and unapproachable as his attitude.

She firmed lips still tingling from that last kiss. "Just stay out of my life," she said with quiet intensity. "I don't need or want your protection." Then she turned and walked away.

CHAPTER THIRTEEN

FOR THE NEXT few days Nate kept telling himself that he'd done the right thing. He didn't have the time or the space in his life for the responsibility of a woman who couldn't—or wouldn't—see how much keeping a promise to his best friend meant to him.

Jack had refused to believe that Nate would grow up to be like his father and even when he'd screw up, his friend would remind him that he wasn't Tom Oliver.

Remind him that he could be anything he wanted.

Well, he'd wanted to be a Navy SEAL, be a part of a something that meant something more—brothers-in-arms fighting for a just cause. It had been a way to earn a few advanced engineering degrees and the pay had helped his mother make ends meet. What he'd never told anyone was that he'd decided it would give him discipline and goals—something his father had lacked.

But the cost had been high. Jack and too many of his brothers-in-arms had paid the ultimate price.

He missed the close bond he'd had with his SEAL team, but he didn't miss having to deal with losing them. Didn't miss having to hold them while they breathed their last.

Yet, even as he told himself he'd done the right thing by keeping his promise to Jack, he couldn't get the look on Frankie's beautiful face out of his head. The quick glint of tears ruthlessly suppressed. The stiff, proud back disappearing out the door.

Almost immediately he'd wanted to stop her because he'd hurt her—something he'd promised himself he'd never do—and when Frankie was hurt she almost always did something reckless.

He'd waited until the next day to call her but she didn't answer or return any of his messages. He went to her house but it was locked up tight and her car was missing. Her partner Dale hadn't heard from her either but, then, he hadn't expected to as they both had a few days off. Nate then called Paige, because if anyone knew where Frankie was it would be the petite doctor. Paige, however, had been quick to deny knowing anything but Nate could tell she was lying. When he called her on it she told him, "I love you but you're an idiot," and disconnected.

Frustrated, he called Ty, whose first words were, "What did you do?"

"Me?" Nate's tone was indignant. "I didn't do anything."

"You must have," Ty said bluntly. "Frankie doesn't just go off without telling anyone."

"Frankie *always* goes off without telling anyone," he reminded him.

"Not anymore. She *always* tells Paige."

"She did tell Paige," Nate pointed out impatiently. "Now, go be a man and get it out of your woman."

"Are you insane?" Ty sounded scandalized. "I prefer sleeping with a soft, warm woman, thank you very much. Go find Frankie yourself and be prepared to beg."

"What the hell, Ty?" Nate swore, frustration beating at his temples because he'd done nothing required him to beg. You'd think people would appreciate the fact that he could keep a promise, that he was a responsible man. Unlike the other men in his family. "You let that sweet little doctor walk all over you?"

"Of course not." His snorted then added in a low voice, "But she says you need to wake up and see what's right under your nose. I'd listen to her, if I were you."

"You're a wuss," Nate said with disgust, but he could hear Ty laughing as his friend disconnected.

Frustrated, he went to work on his deck, needing to finish installing the railings before someone got hurt.

She's already hurt, numbskull.

Yep. He was scum and he felt really bad. Especially now that he knew exactly how she tasted and felt wrapped around him.

He cursed. *Especially* as it wasn't going to happen again.

But if she wanted to go off and sulk, who was he to interfere? She'd told him to stay out of her life and that's exactly what he intended to do. There were plenty of women in town who'd be more than happy to keep him warm at night. Women who weren't wild and reckless and annoying.

Is that what you want? The voice in his head demanded.

"Yes," he said out loud. "That's exactly what I want." But he knew he was lying. Maybe he wouldn't allow himself to think about Frankie but if he was honest with himself, he didn't want to be—couldn't see himself—with any other woman. She'd told him to stay out of her life but that didn't mean he couldn't keep an eye on her from a distance.

Yeah. You're certainly good at distance.

"Shut up," he snarled.

Great. Now he was talking to the voices in his head. Voices that had become as annoying as the woman they were defending.

Maybe he should make an appointment to see a shrink or just get himself committed because he was clearly losing his mind.

So Nate pushed himself, hoping the physical labor would silence the voices and let him sleep without dreaming about Frankie. But working with his hands always left him with far too much time to think, and when a big storm hit the area he moved inside to work on the floor.

With nothing but the sound of the wind and rain, and the monotonous movements of the floor sander, all he *could* do was think.

About Frankie. About the little sounds she made when he was buried deep inside her tight body and the way she'd made sex not just fun but intense. About the way she laughed—completely without artifice and uncaring if people stared. He thought about the way she liked to hog the bed and the way he'd felt with her in his arms.

Like he was where he was meant to be. Like he was the hero she said she didn't want.

"Are you waiting for the carpenter fairies to finish the job or are you mooning over a certain wild redhead who's MIA?"

At the unexpected interruption, Nate's instincts—honed through years of training and combat—reacted with split-second timing. He rose to his feet and spun toward the threat in one smooth move; nail gun locked and loaded for action.

He took one look at Ty lounging in the doorway and cursed. Nate hadn't reacted like that in months, which told him he was losing it. Big time.

And he knew exactly whose fault it was.

Straightening from his combat-ready stance, he lowered his "weapon."

"Do you have a death wish?" he demanded for the second time that week, a bit shaky at the thought that he'd nearly shot his best friend. "I could have nailed you between the eyes a dozen times before you could blink," he growled, shoving one hand through his hair and hoping the surgeon didn't see the fine tremor in his fingers. "Didn't you ever hear about knocking, or announcing your presence? Sneaking up on a SEAL is guaranteed to *seal* your fate."

Ty lifted one dark eyebrow, his bright blue eyes gleaming with amusement. "Wow, I'm impressed," he drawled, brushing raindrops from his dark hair and wandering over to inspect Nate's handiwork. "Two puns in two sentences. And for your information I did knock, *and* call out, but you were too preoccupied with X-rated thoughts."

"Who said they were X-rated?"

"The goofy, lovestruck look said it all."

"I was frowning," Nate pointed out.

Ty dropped down to run his hand over the satin-smooth floorboards. After a couple of beats he looked up and smirked. "Yep, definitely mooning."

Nate snorted and folded his arms across his chest. "I don't moon. Mooning is for saps like you."

"Oh?" Ty straightened, regarding Nate politely. "Is that a Navy SEAL thing or a Nathan Oliver thing?"

"It's a no…thing," Nate growled, dropping his arms and heading for the doorway. "Just minding my own business." He glared over his shoulder when Ty made a scoffing sound. "You want a beer, or what?"

Without waiting for a reply, he stomped into the kitchen and yanked open the refrigerator. By the time he'd pulled out two beers, Ty had joined him. He'd rolled up his sleeves and loosened his tie as though he intended staying a while.

"Why are you here again?" Nate asked, lobbing a beer through the air. Ty snagged it and twisted off the cap with his left hand. The scars on his right hand were still fresh and Nate knew the surgeon was hoping to regain complete use of his hand so he could resume surgery. "Don't you have a fiancée to go irritate?"

"Paige's working, so I thought I'd irritate you instead." He lifted the bottle in a silent toast and took a deep pull, his eyes studying Nate. "It's what buddies do." He swallowed again and licked his lips. "I'd ask what crawled up your ass but since I've been there, I'll give you a piece of advice I wish someone had given me."

Nate gave a rough snort, telling himself that what he was experiencing was a reaction to all the unsolicited advice people kept giving him. It was the only reason his gut burned. The only reason he felt jittery, as though something bad was about to happen. "You're hallucinating, Doc. Probably from sniffing too much happy gas."

"You're a funny guy, Nate," Ty drawled. "But not too bright. At least, not when it comes to Frankie."

"Frankie has nothing to do with this."

"Frankie has *every*thing to do with this but you're just too stubborn to admit it."

Nate casually leaned against the counter and drawled, "Admit what?"

"That you've got it bad and you're too scared to face it."

"What?" He gave a hard laugh and lifted his beer, pointing the bottle at Ty. "That's complete and utter bull, and you know it. I'm not scared, I'm—"

"In love with her." Ty nodded. "Yep, I know."

"Are you out of your freaking mind? I love her, yes. Like a sister. But *in* love?" He made an impatient sound in the back of his throat and shook his head. Because what he felt for Frankie defied description. It couldn't possibly be love.

Could it?

Lust and deep affection, yes...but love? He shook his head emphatically. Nope. No way. "You're insane," he growled, unsure who he was addressing, but just in case it was Ty he added, "I'd have to be certifiable to love a woman like that. She's annoying and opinionated and she makes me crazy."

"Good crazy or bad crazy?"

That's the million-dollar question, isn't it?

He growled, "She frustrates me so much sometimes that I'm tempted to throttle her, so...yep, definitely bad crazy."

Ty's face made it clear he didn't buy it and neither, apparently, did the voice in Nate's head.

You want to wrap your hands around her all right, the voice taunted. *But not to throttle her.*

Ty must have agreed with the voice because he snorted and stared pointedly at Nate. "Yeah…" he smirked "…I can totally see how bad crazy she makes you." He made some kissy noises that ratcheted Nate's annoyance up a couple of hundred notches and made him grit his teeth.

"What are you, twelve?"

Ty snickered before sobering. "It's the best kind of bad, Nate. And if you're really lucky, a woman as fiercely loyal as Frankie comes into your life and has your back."

"Have you forgotten how wild and reckless she is?" Nate demanded, because the thought of him and Frankie…well, it terrified him. "She's a disaster waiting to happen. Just looking out for her is a full-time gig."

"Who says you need to?" Ty asked mildly. "Seems she's done just fine on her own."

The words, spoken by Frankie just a few days earlier, made him scowl. "I don't need that kind of aggravation in my life," he argued curtly.

"Frankie isn't like Paige. She's not a comfortable woman to be around." *Hell*. Just thinking about her made him damned *un*comfortable. The kind of uncomfortable that tempted him to push her up against the nearest wall and put his hands and lips all over her. It was why he needed to stay away from her. "In fact, she can be downright belligerent and…and messy."

Ty grinned. "That's women for you."

Maybe, but Frankie wasn't like other women. She was wild and fiery…and so passionate he had a hard time pushing her from his mind.

His breath whooshed out.

Could he really be in love? With Frankie?

That would be insane and Nate had always prided himself on his cool rationality. But what he felt for Frankie wasn't rational.

Life with her would never be boring. She was too vibrant for that. Too full of life. Too stubborn. They'd fight because she was so…so contrary and opinionated, but the makeup sex would be spectacular.

"*She* saved *your* life, remember?" Ty pointed out, unknowingly slicing to the very heart of what really bothered Nate. Exposing his weakness, his secret shame. "Not the other way around. Or have you forgotten?" Ty demanded. "Because if you have, I still have that video." He pulled out his phone and waggled it. "Wanna see?"

"No. I do not want to see," Nate growled irritably, taking a swig of beer in the hope that it would drown out the sudden realization that he'd resented her for besting him at his own game.

She'd rescued him—instead of the other way around. The way it had always been between them. The way he was comfortable with. He didn't know how to deal with this Frankie, the Frankie who rose without hesitation and threw herself at him. He recalled in perfect detail the horror and devastation in the green eyes locked with his when she'd realized that he was going over; the memory of how her body had felt wrapped around his as they were hoisted into the chopper, and the cuts and bruises she'd sustained saving him.

And not once had she reminded him of it. Not like *he* always seemed to do.

"I don't need to see it to be reminded of that night." He dreamed about it. But in his nightmares their roles were reversed and every time she slipped through his fingers to disappear into the black abyss below. He'd wake drenched in sweat, his heart pounding in his chest and the pain of desolation echoing in his soul.

"The guys at the station remind me often enough, thank you very much."

"Yeah," Ty drawled. "I can see why you'd find that so unsettling."

"What exactly do you mean?" Nate demanded.

"It means that you liked being a SEAL because you got to do all the saving. Frankie's right, you do have a hero complex."

"That's just bull and in case you've forgotten, I'm no longer a SEAL."

"No, you're a coastie. Apples and pears are still fruit, Nate. You're the man sworn to protect and care for everything and everyone around you—your mom, your sister, your country, your teammates… Frankie. It proves to everyone that you're not your father."

"I never had to prove that to anyone," he said curtly, the conversation beginning to really annoy him.

Why, because it's the truth?

"No, just yourself," Ty agreed mildly. *"We've*

always known what you could never see. Just because you share his DNA, it doesn't mean you're going to wake up one morning and suddenly *become* Tom Oliver."

"I know that," Nate snapped, then sighed tiredly. He scrubbed his hands over his face before admitting, "I can't love Frankie... I promised Jack."

Ty's eyebrows shot into his hairline. "You promised him you'd never love her?"

"Buddy rule number one—sisters are off limits. But that's not what I meant," he said wearily. "I promised Jack I'd look out for her—keep her out of trouble. I can't mess with Frankie and keep my promise to Jack."

"Then don't."

"Don't what?" he growled impatiently. "Don't keep my promise? Because I can tell you, I am *not* my father."

"Don't be a moron, Nate. I meant don't *mess* with her."

"But you just said—"

"Jack always knew you loved her," Ty drawled with a glint of amusement.

"Wait. What? She was thirteen, for God's sake. *I* didn't even know I loved her until—"

"You were like brothers," Ty reminded him. "Of course he wanted you to look out for her. But before he died, he knew that you were *in* love with her. He told me."

Nate's jaw dropped open. "*What?* That's cra—"

His instinctive denial was interrupted by Ty's phone.

Ty's mouth curled into a sappy grin as he answered. The look of intimacy, of shared laughter and history told Nate who it was. It also made him feel just a little bit jealous because it was what he wanted too.

And not with just anyone, he finally admitted to himself. He wanted it with Frankie.

She might be wild and unpredictable but she'd always have his back, even—his mouth curled—when she wanted to kill him. She might have saved him from falling off the ledge that night, but he'd gone and fallen anyway.

Hard and completely.

Wham!

He'd been half in love with her for years, but that night...the feel of her against him after so many years, the light of combat in her eyes, the

damn-your-hide attitude…had been like coming home.

Ty was right. Frankie was his heart. She was
the reason he didn't want to spend time with other
women. She was the missing piece of his soul but
he'd been too blinded by his need to prove that he
wasn't like his father—that he could and would
take care of those he loved.

"Babe," Ty's calm voice cut through Nate's
revelation. "Calm down, okay?" His gaze, suddenly unreadable, locked with Nate's but it was
Ty's next words—"Now, what was that about
Frankie?"—that had his blood freezing in his
veins.

He was already reaching for his truck keys and
heading for the front door when Ty ended the
call.

"Before you go off half-cocked, Frankie's fine,"
he said, grabbing his jacket as he followed Nate
out. "She called Paige an hour ago from the ferry
to say a woman was in labor. But Paige said they
just got word that there's been some kind of accident on board and they need all available medics. I'm heading over there to help."

Nate paused. "And Frankie?"

Ty shook his head, his voice steady. "No one's heard from her. But that doesn't mean she's hurt," he added when Nate cursed. "It just means she's probably busy. You know Frankie. She's probably hip-deep in all the action."

But Nate wasn't listening. All he could think about as he dashed through the gusting rain toward his truck was that Frankie was in the hot zone—with no one covering her six. He'd made her believe she was nothing more than a promise to be kept. That he cared more about a memory than a fiery, vibrant woman who owned his heart—and very possibly his soul.

CHAPTER FOURTEEN

ON THE LAST leg of the two-day trip to the local islands, Frankie braced her feet against the pitching deck and tried not to think about the huge waves crashing over the lower decks of the ferry. A huge storm system had hit two days earlier than expected, with gale-force winds whipping the seas into a frenzy. It might not have been so bad if the ferry's stabilizers hadn't been damaged by submerged debris a few hours earlier, rendering the vessel all but unsteerable in the heavy seas.

But right now she had bigger problems than heavy weather and rolling decks. A ferry officer she'd gone to school with had asked her to help out when a man had collapsed, complaining of chest pains and muscle weakness. Then a pregnant woman had gone into early labor and she was soon treating the small band of people injured by the rolling of the ship.

She'd called the hospital to alert them of the emergency—but that had been before lightning had struck, frying all the equipment and starting a fire somewhere in the engine room. Before she'd lost her cellphone when panicked crowds had begun streaming onto the decks, letting rain and sea water pour in through the open doors.

Help was on its way but Frankie had a feeling that time was running out for Serena Porter, who had all the signs of preeclampsia, a dangerous condition for both mother and child.

Then she'd overheard the crew talking about a fire in the cargo bay and had to wonder if they were going down. Smoke had already begun making its way to the upper decks and Frankie prayed help arrived before cars and trucks started exploding.

She also couldn't help hoping that Nate was working on his house and not getting ready to join the rescue. Maybe she was still mad at him for treating her like a one-night stand, but she didn't want him opening up his healing wound.

The knowledge that she was nothing more to him than a responsibility had been a blow to her ego as well as her heart. Discovering that she was in love—a soul-deep connection that throbbed like an open wound—with a man who saw her as just a promise he was honor-bound to keep had devastated her and she'd needed to escape for a while. But running away never solved anything and she couldn't avoid going home forever. Port St. John's wasn't that big and she was bound to run into him sooner rather than later.

Unless she moved to Australia.

Australia had the Great Barrier Reef and she'd always wanted to scuba dive and learn to surf.

"Evac ten minutes out, Miss Bryce," an officer said, popping his head around the door. "Let's get your patients upstairs."

"Upstairs?" Frankie demanded, grateful for the interruption. "I thought they were being airlifted from the port-side deck."

Officer Paul Murray shook his head. "Too many people. The captain is worried they might panic and try to get on the first chopper. We've gotta move your patients to the top observation deck ASAP before we let the rest up there."

Conditions on the upper deck were worse than Frankie had feared. Lightning slashed at the sky, briefly illuminating the wind-driven rain that soaked them instantly. With limited visibility, it took a couple of moments for her to get her bearings and make out the direction of the approaching choppers. Relief had her exhaling in a quiet whoosh when she saw lights appear out of the darkness.

As the nearest chopper lost altitude, figures in protective gear dropped onto the deck and ran toward them, even before the skids made contact. "Medic's waiting in the chopper, Ms. Bryce," someone yelled as they passed. "It's like hell out there, so let's roll."

Paul caught Frankie's shoulder and leaned close to her ear. "I'm going to start directing people up here to the choppers," he said. "Get moving and good luck." Then he was gone.

Frankie quickly ushered the group to the waiting chopper, bending low as rotor wash and lashing rain made it almost impossible to see the hands reaching to pull them to safety. Once the last of her charges was on board, she stepped away and motioned for them to take off.

"You're not coming?" the copilot yelled through the open door. When she shook her head and took a couple more steps back, he lifted his visor.

"Nate said to make sure you got on this chopper," he yelled. "Don't make me go back without you. He knows a hundred ways to kill a man and make it look like an accident."

She rolled her eyes at him but the words stung more than the pelting rain. Even after everything, he was still insisting on being her big brother, her big bad protector?

"Tell the SEAL he's not the boss of me," she yelled back, but as she splashed her way through the torrential rain toward the stairs, she wondered if she would ever get the chance to prove to him that she was worth loving.

"There's been an explosion," the pilot reported abruptly into his comms as they headed back out to the stricken ship, causing Nate's gut to tighten into a fist of dread. "The fuel tanks are starting to explode, so look sharp, men. Those left on board don't have a lot of time."

It was just after eleven and most of the passengers had been airlifted onto waiting coastguard cutters or taken to the medical center, but of Frankie…there was still no word.

Several people had reported seeing her and

Nate had begun to worry that she'd insist on going down with the stricken ship. She'd refused all opportunities to leave with the choppers and wasn't on any of the cutters. He'd checked—countless times—until the shift commander had ordered him to "Get out there and find her, Oliver."

Grateful for the man's understanding, Nate had hopped on the next flight out, hoping Frankie was smart enough to stay out of danger and praying he got the opportunity to tell her how he felt.

They were a few minutes out when another huge fireball ripped through the night sky, briefly illuminating the dangerously listing ship.

"Move in. *Move in,*" he barked into his headset. "Tell them to get the last few people aboard onto the decks so we can evac them now."

He could hear yelling through the comms and saw people spill onto the upper deck. He had time for one horrified thought—*Where the hell is Frankie?*—before finally catching sight of her tearing across the upper deck with several others in pursuit, just as another explosion ripped open the port bulkhead.

They felt the force of it as the chopper slewed sideways and Nate felt terror grip his throat. *"Get *them off. Now!"* he yelled, watching in horror as the ferry lurched sideways, water rushing across the upper deck on which Frankie was scrambling to regain her footing.

He saw dinghies streaking across the water toward the stricken vessel even as people began falling or jumping into the water from the stern.

Frankie and the others were still scrambling up the listing ship, grabbing onto the railings to keep from sliding into the water.

"I'm going in," the pilot yelled, banking sharply to the left. "I'll try to get abreast of their position and hope the rotor wash doesn't sweep them overboard."

"Make sure your lines are secured," Nate ordered as his men scrambled into position. "And get the safety sling ready in case someone doesn't make it."

Ruthlessly squashing the fear that tried to rise up like the angry sea, Nate deliberately slowed his heartbeat and tried to pretend this was just another mission, just another rescue. But as his eyes locked on Frankie with grim determination, he knew he was lying to himself. This wasn't just any rescue. This was about rescuing himself as well.

He caught her expression and knew she understood what they were about to attempt. He saw rather than heard her shouting as the chopper moved in. This close he could see how young they were—probably all ferry staff—and terrified. She shouted, "Jump, they'll catch you," just as another wave broke over them.

The chopper edged closer and one by one the frightened staff were hauled to safety until there was only Frankie and a young uniformed kid left on the deck.

Above the rotor noise, Nate heard another muffled explosion and the next instant the deck pitched dangerously. The pilot jerked the chopper sideways in an attempt to maintain enough rotor distance and Nate saw the kid start to slide. Frankie shouted a warning and shot out her arm to snag the back of his uniform and haul him up.

Eyes white with terror, the kid flailed as he tried to regain his footing as the ferry slid down another few feet.

"She can't hold on forever, LC," the winch operator yelled, tossing a sling at them. It fell short of its mark but Frankie couldn't have grabbed for it anyway. Terrified that they were both going to slide into the churning water, Nate quickly hooked himself to the safety line and scrambled onto the skid. "Give me a little slack," he barked into the comms. "And get as close as you can."

Once the line played out, Nate leaned forward, his arms spread out as though he was flying. Spray from the surging sea instantly covered his visor, making it impossible to see.

Although they were designed to repel water, Nate shoved it up because he couldn't afford to screw up. Not with two lives relying on his experience and training.

Not with Frankie hanging on by one arm while holding onto someone else with the other.

He could literally feel the collective breaths being sucked in behind him as he leaned out over the turbulent water. His gaze locked with Frankie's and all the fear, exhaustion and grim determination in them hit him with a one-two punch.

"Hang on," he yelled, snatching at the swaying rescue sling. "Grab it and if you can, slip it over your head and under your arms. We'll do the rest."

Out the corner of his eye he saw Frankie's face go white with pain and desperately wanted to yell at the kid to hurry up. At the third attempt he managed to snag it and slip it clumsily over his head and under his arms, and Nate finally took his eyes off the kid to shout, "Frankie, let go now and grab my hand."

Eyes on his, her mouth moved and he thought she said *I love you* just as a huge wave broke over her. The sling line abruptly tautened and the boy swung free, jerking at Frankie's body. She wasn't going to be able to hang on against the drag.

"Pull him up and give me four feet," Nate yelled frantically as he watched her struggling against the pull of the water. He instantly felt his line play out and hooked his feet over the chopper floor as he fell forward, catching her just as she lost the battle against the sea.

"I've got you," he said, although he knew she couldn't hear him. Through his comms he heard cheers and, "Oh, my God, he actually did it. Nate's a freaking super bat."

"He's got her, Lieutenant," another voice yelled. "Let's get out of here."

Nate immediately felt the chopper gain altitude before banking sharply away from the sinking ferry.

Using his upper-body strength, he tightened his grip on her arm and pulled her up until she could grab onto his harness.

"You came," she said simply.

And just as simply Nate replied, "Always."

The instant they were hauled aboard, Nate pulled a wet and shivering woman into his arms, only vaguely aware of the excited commotion around them.

He needed a moment. Hell, he needed a whole bunch of moments to get his heart rate down from stroke level and take in the reality of the woman pressed against him. To enjoy the feel of her warm breath on his throat and let the fact that she was alive and safe register. Someone dropped a blanket around her shoulders and after a couple of beats he loosened his grip to wrap it around her icy body.

"I've got you, babe," he murmured, his throat tight and the band of fear around his heart finally loosening. Now that he had her safe he could admit to himself that he'd been scared. Terrified that he would lose the best thing that had ever happened to him.

And looking into her beautiful face he pulled her into his warm body and swore *And this time I'm not letting go.*

After a couple of beats he realized that she was trembling and lifted his head to press his lips against her temple, giving thanks that beneath the delicate skin her pulse beat strong and sure. "You're shaking."

Frankie made a sound between a laugh and a strangled sob. "No," she whispered. "That's you."

It took him a few moments to realize that she was right. He *was* shaking but then again it had been close...too close for comfort.

"I thought I'd lost you," he rasped, pressing his cheek against hers. "I thought..." He sucked in a steadying breath and admitted, "I don't think I'd survive losing you too. Not you, Frankie."

"Hey," she said, pushing back a couple of inches to take his face between her icy palms. "I'm here. I'm not going anywhere."

"You're right," he said firmly. "You're not, but—"

"You saved me," she insisted gently. "Just like you promised Jack. But it's over now, Nate. I'm safe and your debt is paid. Let it go. Let *him* go… It's time."

Hell if she wasn't right. Jack would never be forgotten but maybe it was time to let go of the past, let go of the grief and the guilt of being the one to survive when Jack, the best of them, had died.

"Yes," he admitted, taking her icy hands in his and pressing them against his heart. "And it's also time for you to stop giving me heart failure." He gave a rough laugh. "I can't take much more."

"Me?" she croaked, as though her vocal cords had seized. "What about you?" Huge green eyes glowed eerily in her white face. "What was that? What the heck was that move?"

Now that she was safe and they'd come to terms with Jack's death, he could smile. "Admit it, that move was awesome."

"No," she practically snarled. "It wasn't. It was reckless and stupid and—"

No longer able to keep his relief and joy under wraps, Nate started laughing and quickly dropped a kiss on her surprised mouth, effectively silencing her. "Exactly what you would have done. It's what SEALs call thinking on your feet," he drawled, lowering his voice. "It's what's called being creative and doing whatever you need to do to save the woman you love."

"Well, I call it male stupidity," Frankie said, with a lot less heat. "What were you thinking? What if your line had snapped? What if…?" Her eyes grew huge and she sucked in a shocked breath. "Wha— What did you say?" she whispered hoarsely.

"You heard me. I love you, so damn much. And as to what I was thinking?" he murmured, abruptly serious. "I was thinking that I can't seem to live without you. I was thinking that maybe you were right and I was using my promise to Jack as an excuse to keep you from getting too close." He sucked in a deep breath. "But it's too late. You're already so deep nothing short of a soul transplant will get rid of you."

Frankie looked as though someone had punched her in the head. "You…you l-love me?" she whispered, looking more stunned and vulnerable than he'd ever seen her.

"Hell, yes," Nate declared emphatically, pulling

her against him and tucking her face against his neck. He waited until she lifted her head to say, "I love you, Frankie. With everything that's in me. Seems like I've always loved you, even when you're mean and bossy and drive me completely insane. Besides…" he chuckled when she pushed him lightly "…who else will put up with you?"

A snort of laughter filled the silence. "You might be a superhero, Nate," someone said. "But you sure need lessons in romance."

He caught her hands and lifted them to his mouth. "I'm not the most romantic guy, Frankie, but you're my happy. Without you I'm only just going through the motions."

"Oh, wow," one of the woman survivors sniffed. "If that's not romantic, I don't know what is."

Frankie's hands rose to cup his face. "I don't need romance, Nate," she said, eyes shining with tears and laughter. "I just… I just need you."

"And you'll do as I say?"

Frankie snorted rudely and to Nate it was the most beautiful sound he'd ever heard. Frankie was everything he needed; everything he'd ever wanted, wrapped up in silky-soft skin and prickly attitude. His heart.

"As if, Commander Big Shot," she scoffed. "But," she added when he opened his mouth to object, "I will if you will."

"Be mine," Nate said, oblivious to the whoops and sighs around them.

With a laugh, Frankie yanked him closer, and just before her mouth took his in a passionate kiss she murmured against his lips, "I already am."

* * * * *

LET'S TALK

Romance

For exclusive extracts, competitions and special offers, find us online:

- facebook.com/millsandboon
- @millsandboonuk
- @millsandboon

Or get in touch on 0844 844 1351*

For all the latest titles coming soon, visit millsandboon.co.uk/nextmonth

Want even more
ROMANCE?

Join our bookclub today!

'Mills & Boon books, the perfect way to escape for an hour or so.'

Miss W. Dyer

'Excellent service, promptly delivered and very good subscription choices.'

Miss A. Pearson

'You get fantastic special offers and the chance to get books before they hit the shops'

Mrs V. Hall

Visit millsandbook.co.uk/Bookclub and save on brand new books.

MILLS & BOON